DAWN of the DRAGONWOLF

THREE ADVENTURES COMPATIBLE WITH FIFTH EDITION

Based on *Ranger's Odyssey*, Dragonwolf Trilogy Book One

H. T. MARTINEAU

authorHOUSE®

AuthorHouse™
1663 Liberty Drive
Bloomington, IN 47403
www.authorhouse.com
Phone: 833-262-8899

Interior illustrations: Heidi Thompson
Interior maps and line drawings: H. T. Martineau

Published by AuthorHouse 04/17/2023

ISBN: 979-8-8230-0516-6 (sc)
ISBN: 979-8-8230-0515-9 (e)

Library of Congress Control Number: 2023906399

Print information available on the last page.

This book is printed on acid-free paper.

For the players of AD&D who played with their kids
and cultivated the love of the game in future generations.

Daldar
Dammit
Fanny
Garon
Magnorac
Mayzar

The strongest adventuring party is a family at the tabletop.
I love you all.

CONTENTS

Introduction

Dawn of the Dragonwolf is a trilogy of tabletop adventures set in the world of Ambergrove and following the events of *Ranger's Odyssey*. Adventures are compatible with Dungeons & Dragons fifth edition (5e). All D&D materials mentioned are included under the Creative Commons license. Ambergrove, *Ranger's Odyssey*, and all characters and their distinctive likenesses are property of H. T. Martineau.

The Ambergrove adventures are designed for three to five third-level characters and a Dungeon Master. Players with more experienced characters can adjust character level or use a pregenerated character from the book (included).

This adventure takes place around the world of Ambergrove as the titular character in the first book in the Dragonwolf trilogy, goes from the village of Aeunna to various places across Ambergrove to undergo trial requirements. Two adventures follow Mara, and a third, shorter adventure follows her father, Toren, on his own Ranger trial outside the village of Modoc.

The greatest hurdle for many players in this age of Ambergrove is that there is no magic. A poison has seeped into Ambergrove and stripped the whole world of its magic—even the gods and goddesses. This is a temporary darkness; the Age of Magic begins near the end of the Dragonwolf trilogy. Until then, there are restrictions in place. These are outlined along with other play information here.

Ambergrove vs. 5e

One could sail around the world in forty days with all favorable winds. Some of the travel time is based on help or hindrance of the gods. As indicated by the measurement bar on the map, about the width of the "Aeunna" text on the map is one week walking, one day by horse/wagon, or a half day sailing, not factoring in terrain or divine factors.

Currency is inconsistent or nonexistent in Ambergrove during this time, so for the purpose of the game, use standard 5e systems.

Monster data is included in this book for each encounter. Use the data in this book for enemies rather than your own resources. Monster data—particularly that of the kraken—has been modified to match the story, despite the skewed difficulty levels from standard monsters. **Do NOT throw a standard 5e kraken at your poor Ambergrovian adventurers!** Modified Monster/enemy data is identified by a ✥ when it appears.

This is not your typical 5e campaign or one shot. Ambergrove is its own world with its own systems. While many of those align with standard 5e systems, just as many do not.

There are five modified Ambergrovian elements, with data included for reference.

- Races: **There are six playable races at this time—Bearkin, Forest Dwarf, Gnome, Human, Mining Dwarf, and Sea Elf.** Full race data has been included for each.
- Classes: Because this is a world without magic—for now—there are class restrictions and differences from standard 5e. Approved classes and "spells" are included with modified data to adhere to a magicless world. Some other revisions are made simply to adhere to Ambergrovian culture, such as the addition of new subclasses or modification of the Monk class to Naadakh class. **There are eight approved classes at this time—Barbarian, Bard, Cleric, Fighter, Naadakh, Paladin, Ranger, and Rogue.** Modified class data is included.
- Deities: Ambergrove has its own pantheon. Names and duties are loosely based on the Elder Futhark. There are twelve gods and twelve goddesses in the Ambergrovian pantheon, and their basic information is included.
- Premade PCs: A total of seven premade player character data is included based on the two parties in the most recent Ranger trials. These characters have been assigned classes based on the above modifications and have been leveled to 3rd for those adventurers.
- Magical Items: A shortlist of approved magical items has been included. Pulled from the 5e master list under the Creative Commons license, these have all been modified to eliminate true magic from them so they can exist in Ambergrove in this time. Some is based on Earth technology and some is just oversimplified.

Again, most monster data has been adjusted from 5e references to match *Ranger's Odyssey*. As such, creatures that low-level players typically could not defeat have been included in the story—because it's foremost a *story*, but those changes may not apply to future Ambergrove adventures.

The three adventures included follow the main campaign-like events of the Ranger trials in *Ranger's Odyssey*.

- Session 1: Skipping the forest dwarf trial, this session begins when Mara sets off from Aeunna with her companions. Split into three parts, it includes Mara's first battle from the book, some modified information for the sake of adventure, and ends when she completes her gnome trial after facing a nest of spiderlings and their mother. This follows the second quarter of *Ranger's Odyssey*.
- Session 2: Rearranging some details and modifying others, this three-part adventure focuses on the water. In the second leg of the journey, the party must repair their ship, facing icy beasts, the ice kraken, and running the Serpent's Gauntlet to complete the sea elf trial. This follows the third quarter of *Ranger's Odyssey*.
- Session 3: This session follows Mara's father, Toren, whose Ranger trial is briefly relayed to Mara by her uncle Teddy the day Mara meets the Oracle in the first quarter of *Ranger's Odyssey*. This is a shorter, one-part adventure that is a follows a simple dungeon format.

Preparing the Adventure

As Dungeon Master for these adventures, consider the following.

- Consider familiarizing yourself with the book, *Ranger's Odyssey*. For affordable reading, the book is available for $3.99 in ebook formats in leading online stores, $4.00 in audiobook format from the Tales of Ambergrove website store, and free to borrow on Hoopla. Check local library listings for physical copy availability.
- Read through the adventures you intend to play with your group. If you have any questions after going through things, feel free to reach out to the author through the contact page on the website.
- When you're ready to prepare, familiarize yourself with the encounter materials pertaining to your selected adventure, Ambergrovian structure in the following chapter, and the map of Ambergrove.
- Gather any additional resources for your play style. Maps may be downloaded for presentation or modification by scanning the QR code below.
- Be sure to make necessary adjustments for players beforehand. If players will be creating their own characters, be sure to send them necessary materials about Ambergrove and character restrictions or allow for character creation time on the day. If players will be using pregenerated characters, have them select their characters and give them the character sheets beforehand so they may review—or allow them to copy from this book to a handwritten character sheet.

These are intended to be simple adventures that can be played by individuals who may be inexperienced with or entirely new to D&D. Experienced players can reuse low-level characters or create unique characters if they do not wish to use characters from the book.

If players are using their own characters, check to make sure that all items and monies are appropriate for the PC level. Third is recommended. Spell selection—if you are bypassing the no-magic rule—and other daily character options should be determined before the adventure begins. If you know your players, you may certainly guide them in selecting weapons, spells, or classes best suited to this adventure.

To align with the story, adventures one and two should include a human or forest dwarf ranger, another human or forest dwarf, a gnome, and an elf. Adventure three should include a human or forest dwarf ranger and a human.

> **Note:** Whether players use pregenerated characters or their own, one character <u>must</u> be a ranger.

Adjusting the Adventure

Throughout the adventure, there will be a few adjustments in encounters to allow for smaller or larger groups / higher or lower levels. Use your best judgement. Expected group is 3–5 third-level players.

You know your players best, and you have your own style. Any games can be personalized or optimized. As mentioned in the previous section, there is only one adjustment that cannot be made.

The overall goal of the adventures are for the party leader—of Ranger class—to complete a "Ranger trial." Any other classes may be player's choice. Races selected may be what the players consider the closest equivalent or player preference.

The core duty of the DM is to guide the players on an adventure that is enjoyable. Some narratives will be provided either in this guide or in *Ranger's Odyssey*, but a lot is always up to the DM.

Just remember:

- Use your best judgement. If something isn't working with your group, if things are too easy or too difficult, take a step back and make adjustments.
- Keep things moving. Give players hints when needed and watch for loss of momentum or speed-runs. If you know your players will need help or expect them to want more encounters than included, figure those things in. These are intended as standalone adventures, but they should still be enjoyable sessions on their own or together.
- Just because there is one Ranger does not mean there is one important character. The events have been adjusted to allow for additional companions.

If you have rules for characters you typically add to your games, be sure to include them.

Such as:

- Handling of character death or disease
- Downtime
- Replenishing resources
- Passage of time character elements
- DM rewards

If you're an experienced DM, you do you. If you're new to the role, consider checking out some streams online, checking in with your regular DM (if you have one), or perusing the 5e core books.

Without further ado, Ambergrove awaits!

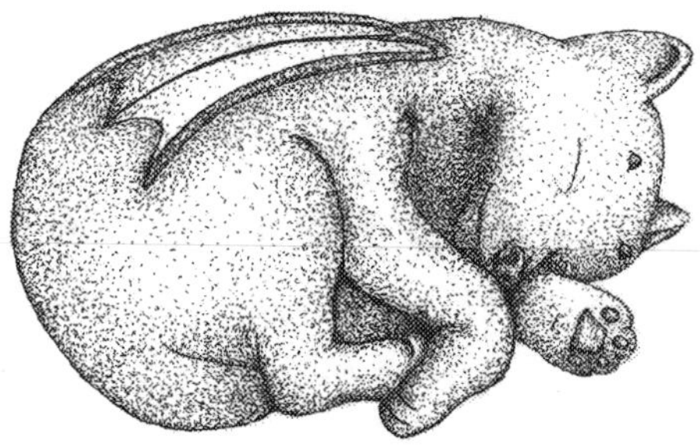

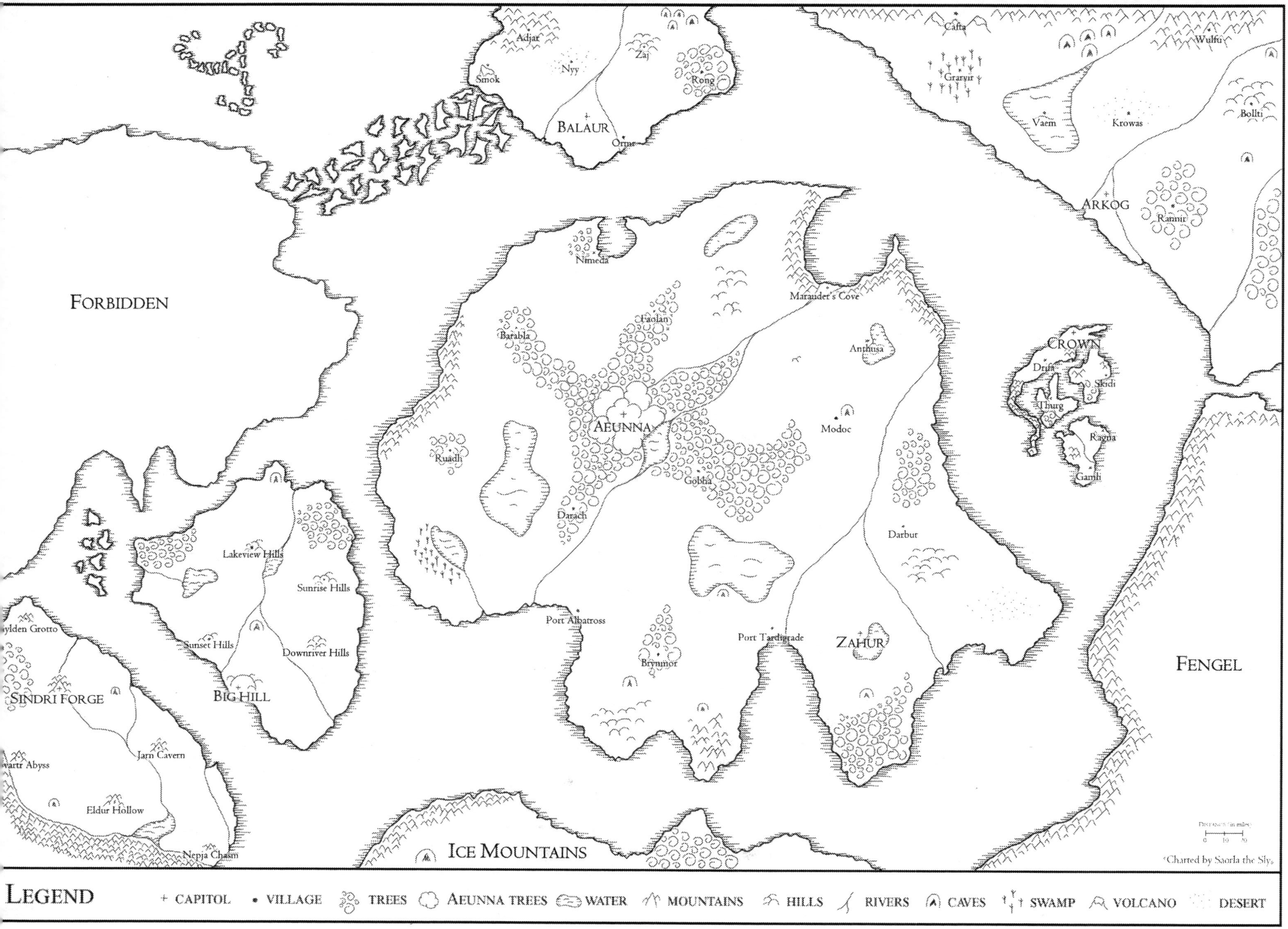
Adjar
Smok
Nyy
Zaj
Rong
Balaur
Ormr
Cafta
Grarvir
Wulfu
Vaem
Krowas
Bollti
Arkog
Ramir
Forbidden
Nimeda
Faolan
Barabla
Marauder's Cove
Anthusa
Crown
Drifa
Skidi
Thurg
Ragna
Gamli
Aeunna
Modoc
Ruadh
Gobha
Darach
Darbut
Lakeview Hills
Sunrise Hills
Port Albatross
Port Tardigrade
Zahur
Fengel
Sunset Hills
Downriver Hills
Brynmor
Big Hill
Sindri Forge
Jarn Cavern
Eldur Hollow
Nepja Chasm
Ice Mountains
Charted by Saorla the Sly
Legend
+ Capitol
• Village
Trees
Aeunna Trees
Water
Mountains
Hills
Rivers
Caves
Swamp
Volcano
Desert

Ambergrove

Created by author H. T. Martineau, Ambergrove is a fantasy world with a connection to Earth. The basic premise is that because the worlds are linked, what we know of fantasy is incomplete. All we know is what has filtered through in the centuries that people have traveled between worlds.

The most significant of these differences pertains to the unique race called *forest dwarves.* D&D has a few different types of dwarves, and the commonality is the similarity to the typical fantasy dwarf. In Ambergrove, these dwarves are called mining dwarves. The idea is that knowledge of mining dwarves seeped through when that of forest dwarves did not. The commonality between the dwarves isn't their stockiness and deep-dwelling as much as their strength. Forest dwarf males are bearded, as are mining dwarf males. Forest dwarves are tall, more akin to orcs or hobgoblins in 5e, growing tall like the trees they inhabit—"short" ones are about six foot. We only know of the typical fantasy dwarves because what we know of dwarves is incomplete, simply coming from previous travelers.

Many of the cultural elements are pulled from ancient civilizations on Earth—Native American, Māori, Ancient Egyptian, Mongolian, Viking, Pictish, Celtic, Ancient Greek, Persian—and many fantasy elements translate as well.

This chapter covers playable races and acceptable classes based on *Ranger's Odyssey* and Ambergrove's full pantheon. For more background information, check out the Tales of Ambergrove website or read the books.

Throughout this book, whenever specific data requires further identification, whether it's added data, data specific to the book, or something new entirely, a ✥ will be used, with its purpose identified at the start of that section.

Playable Races

The mainland is most diverse, due mainly to its size and the temperament of the forest dwarves. As the races of Ambergrove were corrupted by Earth, each began to war with each other and pull away, secluding themselves in their own lands. As such, they each have unique and separate cultures in lands perfectly catered to them.

While more races are introduced in each series, included are playable races as of *Ranger's Odyssey*. Any data modified from 5e is indicated by a ❉ symbol.

Two key elements of 5e race data are not included in Ambergrovian race data.

Age

The age entry notes the age when a member of the race is considered an adult, as well as the race's expected lifespan. This information can help you decide how old your character is at the start of the game. You can choose any age for your character, which could provide an explanation for some of your ability scores. For example, if you play a young or very old character, your age could explain a particularly low Strength or Constitution score, while advanced age could account for a high Intelligence or Wisdom.

❉ However, whereas 5e and many other fantasy worlds have races with all different lifespans—most commonly the elves who live thousands of years—Ambergrovian playable race lifespans are a lot simpler. The oldest of any race is still under 200 years, and maturation is akin to medieval times. Many youths begin gaining adult responsibilities in their early teens.

Languages

❉ In 5e, by virtue of your race, your character can speak, read, and write certain languages. In Ambergrove, everyone speaks Common because there is no other. No indication of language ability is needed unless you are including languages from Earth that are known by descendants of travelers, such as Gaelic, Algonquian, or even still-common languages like Spanish, German, or French.

Other than those two elements, all racial data is included as would be seen in the core books. While some races have obvious links to standard races, such as Mining Dwarves to standard Dwarves, there are two entirely invented races that have a simple model from standard races:

- Bearkin are modified from Halfling data.
- Forest dwarves are modified from Half-orc data.

Bearkin

Bearkin are toddler-sized, bipedal bears with opposable thumbs. Bearkin live on the forest floor of Aeunna in caves at the roots of the Aeunna trees. They are a peaceful people who love food and comfort above all else. They have an understanding with the forest dwarves, and the two races live in harmony. The forest dwarves protect the bearkin, and the bearkin cook for them.

Their names are [tree type] + [tree part]. (Mapleleaf, Ashroot, Tuliptwig, etc.)

Your bearkin character has a number of traits in common with all other bearkin.

Ability Score Increase. Your Constitution score increases by 2.

Alignment. Most bearkin are lawful good or lawful neutral. As a rule, they are good-hearted and kind, hate to see others in pain, and have no tolerance for oppression. They are also very orderly and traditional, leaning heavily on the support of their community and the comfort of their homely ways.

Size. Halflings average about 3 feet tall and weigh about 50 pounds. Your size is Small.

Speed. Your base walking speed is 25 feet.

Lucky. When you roll a 1 on the d20 for an attack roll, ability check, or saving throw, you can reroll the die and must use the new roll.

Bear Step. You can move through the space of any creature that is of a size larger than yours. As a bearkin, you can easily hide from notice, even using other people as cover.

But a Babe. You simply appear to others as a bear cub rather than a bearkin unless you walk as a humanoid or speak to them.

Peaceful. You're inclined to be affable and get along well with others. You have a disadvantage in melee combat.

Lick the Spoon. You have advantage on saving throws against poison.

Standard Gear Bearkin as a race of cooks all have *cooks' utensils* and a *mess kit* among their supplies.

GNOMES

Gnomes live in the southwest of Ambergrove, tucked in the shadow of the forbidden lands. This keeps them safe from many of the other marauders, as not even the dangerous dare venture into those lands. They live in and around the hills of this land and are afraid of most of the other creatures in Ambergrove. They do not get along with much of anyone, either when others visit or when they venture out—particularly the mining dwarves. Gnomes are often dismissed as simply the "soft" version of mining dwarves, and that may have led to some of the unrest between the two. Gnomes blend in with the hills for their own safety, and pureblooded gnomes are the colors of the earth.

Their names all include G, K, or L and are no more than two syllables in length (Gaetan, Kip, Kina, Loli, Sokti).

Your gnome character has certain characteristics in common with all other gnomes.

Ability Score Increase. Your Intelligence score increases by 2 and your Constitution score increases by 1.

Alignment. Gnomes are most often good. Those who tend toward law are guards, paladins, or healers. Those who tend toward chaos are minstrels, tricksters, or barbarians, despite their size. Gnomes are good-hearted, and even the tricksters among them are more playful than vicious.

Size. Gnomes are between 4 and 5 feet tall and average about 80 pounds. Your size is Small.

Speed. Your base walking speed is 25 feet.

Darkvision. Accustomed to life underground, you have superior vision in dark and dim conditions. You can see in dim light within 60 feet of you as if it were bright light, and in darkness as if it were dim light. You can't discern color in darkness, only shades of gray.

Gnome Cunning. You have advantage on all Intelligence, Wisdom, and Charisma saving throws.

Crafter's Lore. Whenever you make an Intelligence (History) check related to crafted tools, you can add twice your proficiency bonus, instead of any proficiency bonus you normally apply.

Whittler or Sculptor. You have proficiency with artisan's tools pertaining to wood or stone, but not both. Using those tools, you can spend 1 hour and the required wooden or stone materials to construct a Tiny carved or sculpted tool (AC 5, 1 hp). Single use only; for distraction or use.

When you create a tool, choose one of the following options:

Carven Creature. This toy is a carved or sculpted animal, monster, or person, such as a frog, mouse, bird, dragon, or soldier. You may present it to an NPC for a Charisma bonus toward whoever you gave it to.

Toolmaker. Create a small mallet, axe, or other simple tool from wood or stone. Using the device requires your action. If used as a weapon, use a simple club for damage data.

Adept Toss. With chosen material, the gnome may toss a stick or stone with advantaged precision to cause a distraction, spring a trap, or for a similar use at DM's discretion.

Standard Gear A Whittler will have *woodcarver's tools* and a Sculptor will have *mason tools* among their supplies.

Forest Dwarves

The forest dwarves are unique to Ambergrove, and their capitol is Aeunna. Other villages are nestled in forested areas in the mainland, all with Celtic inspired names. The nature of the travel between Earth and Ambergrove over the centuries meant that many misconceptions made their way through. The mining dwarves were all that Earthers thought of, because forest dwarves were barely discernable from humans. When the tales were passed on through the centuries, those from Earth assumed that all dwarves were small because of the mining dwarves. The forest dwarves have the same general look as the mining dwarves—burly and muscled, and the men are bearded—but whereas the mining dwarves' size allows them to delve into smaller caverns in the mountains, the forest dwarves grow tall like trees. Forest dwarves are nature-driven gentle giants. The pureblooded forest dwarves have hair and skin of greens, browns, and reds—colors of the forest.

Their names are mostly Celtic or Old Norse inspired. Otherwise, they are inspired by the forest.

Your forest dwarf character has certain traits deriving from your forest dwarf ancestry.

Ability Score Increase. Your Strength score increases by 2, and your Constitution score increases by 1.

Alignment. Forest dwarves inherit a tendency toward good from their care of the forest around them. They are raised to protect the forest and its creatures as well as the natural world as a whole.

Size. Forest dwarves are somewhat larger and bulkier than humans, and they range from 6 to well over 8 feet tall. Your size is Medium.

Speed. Your base walking speed is 30 feet.

Menacing. You gain proficiency in the Intimidation skill due to height and build.

Animal Speech. All forest dwarves have the ability to talk with any creatures that have the intelligence and temperament to communicate, regardless of class.

Call of the Forest. You are able to identify and determine simple use of any plant or creature native to the forest.

Barkskin. When you are reduced to 0 hit points but not killed outright, you can drop to 1 hit point instead. You can't use this feature again until you finish a long rest.

Lumberjack. When you score a critical hit with a melee weapon attack, you can roll one of the weapon's damage dice one additional time and add it to the extra damage of the critical hit.

Humans

Humans share the mainland with the forest dwarves. Their capitol is Zahur. Each human village is inspired by a different culture from ancient Earth. The humans—and those of human blood who may pass as fully human—are the only ones who can travel between Earth and Ambergrove. It is through this restriction that all known of Ambergrove on Earth was simply disregarded as fantasy, thus protecting the whole world from the worst of Earth for millennia. It was the humans who first settled in what they called Lesser Earth (now the forbidden lands) and built cities and recreated modernities they missed from Earth. These cities grew out of control, as did their people, and all of Ambergrove broke apart because of it.

Their names depend greatly on the town of origin.

- **Zahur:** Persian and Ancient Egyptian
- **Modoc:** Ancient Greek/Roman (formerly Native American)
- **Nimeda:** Native American
- **Darbut:** Aboriginal
- **Anthusa:** Mongolian and other East Asian

As a human born in Ambergrove or returned to it, your character has these traits.

Ability Score Increase. Your ability scores each increase by 1.

Alignment. Humans tend toward neutrality or chaos in any form.

Size. Humans vary widely in height and build, from nearly 4 feet to well over 6 feet tall. Regardless of your position in that range, your size is Medium.

Speed. Your base walking speed is 30 feet.

Subrace: Earther

As someone of Ambergrovian blood, you grew up somewhere on Earth, but it was never your home. Even so, you are able to benefit from your Earthly knowledge. When you create your character, you must choose a time period and location on which to base your character's additional expertise. Keep in mind, characters come to Ambergrove from Earth at age sixteen. You must be at least sixteen and you cannot know more about the world than a sixteen-year-old would know in your selected Earthly period and region.

Sample Earther Origins:

- From Old West Texas, your father was a general store owner. You know a lot about supplies and their uses. You grew up in a time of gunslingers and learned how to shoot before you lost your first baby tooth
- From the Mongol Dynasty, you grew up an urchin near one of Genghis Khan's encampments and were then raised by his advisers. You learned military strategy before you learned to read.
- From 1930s Australia, you are a half-Aboriginal child who was raised to be one with the land. You have an uncanny understanding of the elements around you.

Alien. You have knowledge from Earth and can use that to your advantage a maximum of twice per day. What you can know is at the DM's discretion.

Mining Dwarves

The mining dwarves live in the southwest, further south than even the gnomes. As the gnomes live in the hills, the mining dwarves live in the mountains. They are very similar to the stereotypical dwarves in fantasy. They are a gruff and grumpy people who mostly only get along with their forest kin. As stereotypical fantasy suggests, they are talented smiths, and their mastery of the mountains and their secrets are unparalleled. Pureblooded mining dwarves are the colors of fire and forge—mainly fiery reds, charcoal greys, and cavern blacks.

Their names are similar to those in 5e. Additionally, some have names that pertain to smithing or mining (Ember, Hamr, Ruby, Flint).

Your mining dwarf character has an assortment of inborn abilities, part and parcel of mining-dwarven nature.

Ability Score Increase. Your Constitution score increases by 2.

Alignment. Most dwarves are lawful, believing firmly in the benefits of a well-ordered society. They tend toward good as well, with a strong sense of fair play and a belief that everyone deserves to share in the benefits of a just order. Any who do not contribute to the overall order are cast out.

Size. Dwarves stand between 4 and 5 feet tall and average about 150 pounds. Your size is Medium.

Speed. Your base walking speed is 25 feet. Your speed is not reduced by wearing heavy armor.

Darkvision. Accustomed to life underground, you have superior vision in dark and dim conditions. You can see in dim light within 60 feet of you as if it were bright light, and in darkness as if it were dim light. You can't discern color in darkness, only shades of gray.

Dwarven Combat Training. You have proficiency with the battleaxe, handaxe, light hammer, and warhammer.

Tool Proficiency. You gain proficiency with the artisan's tools of your choice: *smith's tools, brewer's supplies,* or *mason's tools.*

Stonecunning. Whenever you make an Intelligence (History) check related to the origin of stonework, gemology, or smithing, you are considered proficient in the History skill and add double your proficiency bonus to the check, instead of your normal proficiency bonus.

Dwarven Toughness. Your hit point maximum increases by 1, and it increases by 1 every time you gain a level.

Sea Elves

The sea elves live in the cluster of islands to the east in the shape of a sea serpent. They are famed warriors and sailors. Their talents with the seas cause some to think that magic never really left Ambergrove. They live on the back of a rocky serpent and its eggs—or so their tales say. Their ships are crafted in unique blues and greens, blending in with the seawaters completely. The people, too, are the colors of the sea—greens and blues, and some purples, coral, and coral pink. The sea elves are thought by many of the other races to be barbaric, and they are the only ones that require their citizens to complete a trial to avoid banishment at the age of fifteen. Any sea elf who fails to complete the Serpent's Gauntlet and does not perish in the attempt is executed or banished from the sea elves' lands, never to return.

Your character must be of age and have passed the gauntlet. If you have read the book and know why your chances of surviving exiled are virtually nonexistent, you can create your character with that background and means of survival. Although you will have gone through the gauntlet, for the purpose of these adventures, you are unable to remember how—so you cannot use your knowledge to complete it again or help another.

Their names always have something to do with the sea. Some are named after fish or fish parts (Candiru, Finn), some ship components (Brig, Anchor), some geographical sea elements (River, Reef, Shoal), and some simply sealike colors.

As one of the famed sea elves, your character has these traits.

Ability Score Increase. Your Dexterity score increases by 2 and your Intelligence score increases by 1.

❁ **Alignment.** Elves value the warrior and are often self-serving. Alignment is determined by universal perception, so they lean strongly toward evil for the barbarism alone. Those who reject the societal ways are more neutral or chaotic.

Size. Elves range from under 5 to over 6 feet tall and have slender builds. Your size is Medium.

Speed. Your base walking speed is 30 feet.

Darkvision. Accustomed to twilit seas and the night sky, you have superior vision in dark and dim conditions. You can see in dim light within 60 feet of you as if it were bright light, and in darkness as if it were dim light. You can't discern color in darkness, only shades of gray.

Keen Senses. You have proficiency in the Perception skill.

❁ **Marauder.** You are a proficient sailor and are adept at all nautical arts.

❁ **Confidence.** You are haughty and determined, believing yourself to be superior to non-elves and even other elves.

❁ **Elf Weapon Training.** You have proficiency with the longsword, longbow, and polearms or spears.

❁ **Standard Gear** Sea elves, as a race of sailors, will all have *navigator's tools* and a *spyglass* among their supplies.

Restricted Classes

Ambergrove in Toren and Mara's time is a world without magic. The western landmass in Ambergrove is referred to in their time as the forbidden lands, due to the corruption and evil long bred there. It is a hub of science and modernity. As more science made its way into Ambergrove and the corruption took over, magic began to filter out of the land until even the gods and goddesses were unable to use their magic except in utmost need. Science is man's way of creating magic where there is none, so it drives true magic away.

Ashroot is a cleric for the purpose of this game, because she is the one who makes the poultices and healing teas perfected by Teddy's lifemate (wife), Freya, so her use of healing spells, along with other "magic" that could be explained, remains to preserve popular classes.

Only few spells are permissible, and those are the ones that can be explained away as not magical. Use the included class data instead of your typical 5e resource. Besides those included in this book, no other magic users or magical items would be present in this world at this time. **You may ignore this rule if you wish and simply use 5e.**

Additionally, as is repeated a few times throughout, the point of these sessions is for a Ranger of Aeunna to complete the Ranger trial and prove themselves leader of the forest dwarves. As such, at least one player must be of the Ranger class.

You may alter any details you would like regarding races or classes except the inclusion of a Ranger character. Some Ranger elements are necessary for completion.

Barbarian

As a barbarian, you gain the following class features.

Hit Points

Hit Dice: 1d12 per barbarian level
Hit Points at 1st Level: 12 + your Constitution modifier
Hit Points at Higher Levels: 1d12 (or 7) + your Constitution modifier per barbarian level after 1st

Proficiencies

Armor: Light armor, medium armor, shields
Weapons: Simple weapons, martial weapons
Tools: None
Saving Throws: Strength, Constitution
Skills: Choose two from Animal Handling, Athletics, Intimidation, Nature, Perception, and Survival

Equipment

You start with the following equipment, in addition to the equipment granted by your background:

- (a) a greataxe or (b) any martial melee weapon
- (a) two handaxes or (b) any simple weapon
- (a) an explorer's pack and four javelins

The Barbarian

Level	Proficiency Bonus	Features	Rages	Rage Damage
1	+2	Rage, unarmored defense	2	+2
2	+2	Reckless attack, danger sense	2	+2
3	+2	Primal path	3	+2
4	+2	Ability Score Improvement	3	+2
5	+3	Extra attack, fast movement	3	+2
6	+3	Path feature	4	+2
7	+3	Feral instinct	4	+2
8	+3	Ability Score Improvement	4	+2
9	+4	Brutal Critical (1 die)	4	+3
10	+4	Path feature	4	+3
11	+4	Relentless rage	4	+3
12	+4	Ability Score Improvement	5	+3
13	+5	Brutal Critical (2 dice)	5	+3
14	+5	Path feature	5	+3
15	+5	Persistent rage	5	+3
16	+5	Ability Score Improvement	5	+4
17	+6	Brutal Critical (3 dice)	6	+4
18	+6	Indomitable might	6	+4
19	+6	Ability Score Improvement	6	+4
20	+6	Primal Champion	Unlimited	+4

Rage

In battle, you fight with primal ferocity. On your turn, you can enter a rage as a bonus action. While raging, you gain the following benefits if you aren't wearing heavy armor:

- You have advantage on Strength checks and Strength saving throws.
- When you make a melee weapon attack using Strength, you gain a bonus to the damage roll that increases as you gain levels as a barbarian, as shown in the Rage Damage column of the Barbarian table.
- You have resistance to bludgeoning, piercing, and slashing damage.

Your rage lasts for 1 minute. It ends early if you are knocked unconscious or if your turn ends and you haven't attacked a hostile creature since your last turn or taken damage since then. You can also end your rage on your turn as a bonus action.

Once you have raged the number of times shown for your barbarian level in the Rages column of the Barbarian table, you must finish a long rest before you can rage again.

Unarmored Defense

While you are not wearing any armor, your Armor Class equals 10 + your Dexterity modifier + your Constitution modifier. You can use a shield and still gain this benefit.

Reckless Attack

Starting at 2nd level, you can throw aside all concern for defense to attack with fierce desperation. When you make your first attack on your turn, you can decide to attack recklessly. Doing so gives you advantage on melee weapon attack rolls using Strength during this turn, but attack rolls against you have advantage until your next turn.

Danger Sense

At 2nd level, you gain an uncanny sense of when things nearby aren't as they should be, giving you an edge when you dodge away from danger.

You have advantage on Dexterity saving throws against effects that you can see, such as traps and spells. To gain this benefit, you can't be blinded, deafened, or incapacitated.

Primal Path

At 3rd level, you choose a path that shapes the nature of your rage. Choose the Path of the Berserker or the Path of the Protector, both detailed at the end of the class description. Your choice grants you features at 3rd level and again at 6th, 10th, and 14th levels.

Ability Score Improvement

When you reach 4th level, and again at 8th, 12th, 16th, and 19th level, you can increase one ability score of your choice by 2, or you can increase two ability scores of your choice by 1. As normal, you can't increase an ability score above 20 using this feature.

Extra Attack

Beginning at 5th level, you can attack twice, instead of once, whenever you take the Attack action on your turn.

Fast Movement

Starting at 5th level, your speed increases by 10 feet while you aren't wearing heavy armor.

Feral Instinct

By 7th level, your instincts are so honed that you have advantage on initiative rolls.

Additionally, if you are surprised at the beginning of combat and aren't incapacitated, you can act normally on your first turn, but only if you enter your rage before doing anything else on that turn.

Brutal Critical

Beginning at 9th level, you can roll one additional weapon damage die when determining the extra damage for a critical hit with a melee attack.

This increases to two additional dice at 13th level and three additional dice at 17th level.

Relentless Rage

Starting at 11th level, your rage can keep you fighting despite grievous wounds. If you drop to 0 hit points while you're raging and don't die outright, you can make a DC 10 Constitution saving throw. If you succeed, you drop to 1 hit point instead.

Each time you use this feature after the first, the DC increases by 5. When you finish a short or long rest, the DC resets to 10.

Persistent Rage

Beginning at 15th level, your rage is so fierce that it ends early only if you fall unconscious or if you choose to end it.

Indomitable Might

Beginning at 18th level, if your total for a Strength check is less than your Strength score, you can use that score in place of the total.

Primal Champion

At 20th level, you embody the power of the wilds. Your Strength and Constitution scores increase by 4. Your maximum for those scores is now 24.

Path of the Berserker

For some barbarians, rage is a means to an end—that end being violence. The Path of the Berserker is a path of untrammeled fury, slick with blood. As you enter the berserker's rage, you thrill in the chaos of battle, heedless of your own health or well-being.

Frenzy

Starting when you choose this path at 3rd level, you can go into a frenzy when you rage. If you do so, for the duration of your rage you can make a single melee weapon attack as a bonus action on each of your turns after this one. When your rage ends, you suffer one level of exhaustion.

Mindless Rage

Beginning at 6th level, you can't be charmed or frightened while raging. If you are charmed or frightened when you enter your rage, the effect is suspended for the duration of the rage.

Intimidating Presence

Beginning at 10th level, you can use your action to frighten someone with your menacing presence. When you do so, choose one creature that you can see within 30 feet of you. If the creature can see or hear you, it must succeed on a Wisdom saving throw (DC equal to 8 + your proficiency bonus + your Charisma modifier) or be frightened of you until the end of your next turn. On subsequent turns, you can use your action to extend the duration of this effect on the frightened creature until the end of your next turn. This effect ends if the creature ends its turn out of line of sight or more than 60 feet away from you.

If the creature succeeds on its saving throw, you can't use this feature on that creature again for 24 hours.

Retaliation

Starting at 14th level, when you take damage from a creature that is within 5 feet of you, you can use your reaction to make a melee weapon attack against that creature.

Path of the Protector

For other barbarians, that end is helping others. The Path of the Protector is a path of one who is blinded by rage when the defenseless are in danger. As you enter the protector's rage, you are consumed by the need to eliminate the threats to the weak, heedless of your own health or well-being.

Human Shield

Starting when you choose this path at 3rd level, you can earn a bonus action when you rage. You can move to stand between an enemy and an ally, regardless of standard speed, shielding the ally as their protector. You fully block the ally from harm and suffer half damage from any attack that hits during your rage. When your rage ends, you suffer one level of exhaustion.

Mindless Rage

Beginning at 6th level, you can't be charmed or frightened while raging. If you are charmed or frightened when you enter your rage, the effect is suspended for the duration of the rage.

Soothing Presence

Beginning at 10th level, you can use your action to calm someone with your protector's presence. When you do so, choose one creature that you can see within 30 feet of you. If the creature can see or hear you, it must fail on a Wisdom saving throw (DC equal to 8 + your proficiency bonus + your Charisma modifier) or be calmed by you until the end of your next turn. On subsequent turns, you can use your action to extend the duration of this effect on the calmed creature until the end of your next turn. This effect ends if the creature ends its turn out of line of sight or more than 60 feet away from you.

If the creature fails on its saving throw, you can't use this feature on that creature again for 24 hours.

Retaliation

Starting at 14th level, when you absorb melee damage when using Human Shield, you can use your reaction to make a melee weapon attack against the attacker.

Bard

As a bard, you gain the following class features.

Hit Points

Hit Dice: 1d8 per bard level
Hit Points at 1st Level: 8 + your Constitution modifier
Hit Points at Higher Levels: 1d8 (or 5) + your Constitution modifier per bard level after 1st

Proficiencies

Armor: Light armor
Weapons: Simple weapons, hand crossbows, longswords, rapiers, shortswords
Tools: Three musical instruments of your choice or additional materials depending on college of choice.
Saving Throws: Dexterity, Charisma
Skills: Choose any three

Equipment

You start with the following equipment, in addition to the equipment granted by your background:

- (a) a rapier, (b) a longsword, or (c) any simple weapon
- (a) a diplomat's pack or (b) an entertainer's pack
- (a) a lute or (b) any other musical instrument
- (a) leather armor and a dagger

The Bard

Level	Proficiency Bonus	Features
1	+2	Spells, Bardic Inspiration (d6)
2	+2	Jack of All Trades, Song of Rest (d6)
3	+2	Bard College, Expertise
4	+2	Ability Score Improvement
5	+3	Bardic Inspiration (d8), Font of Inspiration
6	+3	Countercharm
7	+3	Spell
8	+3	Ability Score Improvement
9	+4	Song of Rest (d8)
10	+4	Bardic Inspiration (d10), Expertise, Magical Secrets
11	+4	—
12	+4	Ability Score Improvement
13	+5	Song of Rest (d10)
14	+5	Bard College feature
15	+5	Bardic Inspiration (d12)
16	+5	Ability Score Improvement
17	+6	Song of Rest (d12)
18	+6	—
19	+6	Ability Score Improvement
20	+6	Superior Inspiration

Spellcasting

You have learned to untangle and reshape the fabric of reality in harmony with your wishes and music. Your spells are part of your vast repertoire, magic that you can tune to different situations.

❖ However, in the scope of Ambergrove in the Lost Age, "magic" here is not magic at all. A "spell" list is included at the end of the Bard data, detailing the eight total spells permitted to the class during this time. Because these are not truly magic, the typical spell slots do not apply.

❖ You know three cantrips and four 1st-level spells from the standard spell list—with modifications—and you will learn one 7th-level spell.

Spellcasting Ability

❖ Charisma is your spellcasting ability for your bard spells. Your magic comes from the heart and soul you pour into the performance of your music or oration. You use your Charisma whenever a spell refers to your spellcasting ability. In effect, your "magic" is simple illusions of a stage magician's caliber. It's just trickery and misdirection. In addition, you use your Charisma modifier when setting the saving throw DC for a bard spell you cast and when making an attack roll with one.

Spell save DC = 8 + your proficiency bonus + your Charisma modifier

Spell attack modifier = your proficiency bonus + your Charisma modifier

Spellcasting Focus

You can use a *musical instrument, disguise kit,* or other specific bardic item as a spellcasting focus for your bard spells.

Bardic Inspiration

You can inspire others through stirring words or music. To do so, you use a bonus action on your turn to choose one creature other than yourself within 60 feet of you who can hear you. That creature gains one Bardic Inspiration die, a d6.

Once within the next 10 minutes, the creature can roll the die and add the number rolled to one ability check, attack roll, or saving throw it makes. The creature can wait until after it rolls the d20 before deciding to use the Bardic Inspiration die, but must decide before the DM says whether the roll succeeds or fails. Once the Bardic Inspiration die is rolled, it is lost. A creature can have only one Bardic Inspiration die at a time.

You can use this feature a number of times equal to your Charisma modifier (a minimum of once). You regain any expended uses when you finish a long rest.

Your Bardic Inspiration die changes when you reach certain levels in this class. The die becomes a d8 at 5th level, a d10 at 10th level, and a d12 at 15th level.

Jack of All Trades

Starting at 2nd level, you can add half your proficiency bonus, rounded down, to any ability check you make that doesn't already include your proficiency bonus.

Song of Rest

Beginning at 2nd level, you can use soothing music or oration to help revitalize your wounded allies during a short rest. If you or any friendly creatures who can hear your performance regain hit points at the end of the short rest by spending one or more Hit Dice, each of those creatures regains an extra 1d6 hit points.

The extra hit points increase when you reach certain levels in this class: to 1d8 at 9th level, to 1d10 at 13th level, and to 1d12 at 17th level.

Bard College

At 3rd level, you delve into the advanced techniques of a bard college of your choice, such as the College of Lore. Your choice grants you features at 3rd level and again at 14th level.

The features are the same regardless of chosen college. However, your college will affect other elements of gameplay.

Bonus Proficiencies

When you join a college at 3rd level, you gain proficiency with three skills of your choice.

Cutting Words

Also at 3rd level, you learn how to use your wit to distract, confuse, and otherwise sap the confidence and competence of others. When a creature that you can see within 60 feet of you makes an attack roll, an ability check, or a damage roll, you can use your reaction to expend one of your uses of Bardic Inspiration, rolling a Bardic Inspiration die and subtracting the number rolled from the creature's roll. You can choose to use this feature after the creature makes its roll, but before the DM determines whether the attack roll or ability check succeeds or fails, or before the creature deals its damage. The creature is immune if it can't hear you or if it's immune to being charmed.

Peerless Skill

Starting at 14th level, when you make an ability check, you can expend one use of Bardic Inspiration. Roll a Bardic Inspiration die and add the number rolled to your ability check. You can choose to do so after you roll the die for the ability check, but before the DM tells you whether you succeed or fail.

Expertise

At 3rd level, choose two of your skill proficiencies. Your proficiency bonus is doubled for any ability check you make that uses either of the chosen proficiencies.

At 10th level, you can choose another two skill proficiencies to gain this benefit.

Ability Score Improvement

When you reach 4th level, and again at 8th, 12th, 16th, and 19th level, you can increase one ability score of your choice by 2, or you can increase two ability scores of your choice by 1. As normal, you can't increase an ability score above 20 using this feature.

Font of Inspiration

Beginning when you reach 5th level, you regain all of your expended uses of Bardic Inspiration when you finish a short or long rest.

Countercharm

At 6th level, you gain the ability to use musical notes or words of power to disrupt mind-influencing effects. As an action, you can start a performance that lasts until the end of your next turn.

❉ You begin to sing a pre-chosen earworm song—something that gets stuck in your head, distracting yourself or others from ill effects.

During that time, you and any friendly creatures within 30 feet of you have advantage on saving throws against being frightened or charmed. A creature must be able to hear you to gain this benefit. The performance ends early if you are incapacitated or silenced or if you voluntarily end it (no action required).

Superior Inspiration

At 20th level, when you roll initiative and have no uses of Bardic Inspiration left, you regain one use.

❉ College of Lore

Bards of the College of Lore know something about most things, collecting bits of knowledge from sources as diverse as scholarly tomes and peasant tales. Whether telling tales in taverns or elaborate compositions for a lavish event, these bards use their gifts to hold audiences spellbound. When the applause dies down, the audience members might find themselves questioning everything they held to be true.

The loyalty of these bards lies in the pursuit of beauty and truth. The college's members gather in libraries to share their lore with one another. They also meet at festivals or affairs of state, where they can expose corruption, unravel lies, and poke fun at self-important figures of authority.

You are granted a Charisma bonus when telling a story.

❉ Standard Gear

Bards of the College of Lore have one *musical instrument* among their supplies.

❉ College of Song

Bards of the College of Song specialize in the use of music to enthrall others. They are one with their chosen instrument, can play any tune by ear, and always sing on key. When the applause dies down, the audience members might find themselves questioning everything that is important.

The loyalty of these bards lies in the muse and melody. The college's members gather in pubs, inns, and village squares, as well as festivals and carnivals. They go where the music is.

You are granted a Charisma bonus when singing or playing your chosen instrument.

❉ Standard Gear

Bards of the College of Song have one *musical instrument* among their supplies.

❉ College of Wit

Bards of the College of Wit are jokesters and jerks. They specialize in the art of comedy, often at others' expense. Audience members may laugh at the bard's jokes or groan at the zinger delivered at another's expense.

The loyalty of these bards is nonexistent. They lean toward chaotic alignments and are often distracted by the need to ruffle feathers with their wit. The college's members gather in pubs and crowded areas where their words can make the most impact.

You receive a Charisma bonus when telling jokes or making jabbing remarks.

You must *actually* come up with jokes or zingers in real life and tell them to your party to use this bonus.

Standard Gear

Bards of the College of Wit have a *disguise kit* among their supplies.

College of Hijinx

Bards of the College of Hijinx are master magicians, using their sleight of hand and other skills to use magic performatively where no magic really appears. When the applause dies down, the audience members might find themselves questioning their own reality.

The loyalty of these bards lies in the fun of their illusions.

The college's members gather in the streets where they can use pyrotechnics without the fear of burning down a building.

You receive a Charisma bonus when completing magic tricks.

Standard Gear

Bards of the College of Wit have a *disguise kit* among their supplies.

Restricted Spellbook

Cantrips

Dancing Lights

Evocation cantrip
Casting Time: 1 action
Range: 120 feet
Components: V, S, M (glow stones)
Duration: Concentration, up to 1 minute

You have a pocketful of glow stones you can use to create light and retrieve to reuse by simply picking them up where they fall. Each light sheds dim light in a 5-foot radius.

As a bonus action on your turn, you can move the lights up to 60 feet to a new spot within range. A light must be within 20 feet of another light created by this spell, and a light winks out if it exceeds the spell's range.

Minor Illusion

Illusion cantrip
Casting Time: 1 action
Range: 30 feet
Components: S, M (something pertaining to the visual)
Duration: 1 minute

You create a sound or an image of an object within range that lasts for the duration. The illusion also ends if you dismiss it as an action or cast this spell again.

If you create a sound, its volume can range from a whisper to a scream. It can be your voice, someone else's voice, a lion's roar, a beating of drums, or any other sound you choose. You do this by throwing your voice and doing impressions (think Robin Williams). The sound continues unabated throughout the duration, or you can make discrete sounds at different times before the spell ends.

If you create an image of an object, the image can't create sound, light, smell, or any other sensory effect. Physical interaction with the image reveals it to be an illusion, because things can pass through it. It must be something you could feasibly do as a magic trick.

If a creature uses its action to examine the sound or image, the creature can determine that it is an illusion with a successful Intelligence (Investigation) check against your spell save DC. If a creature discerns the illusion for what it is, the illusion becomes faint to the creature.

❁ Vicious Mockery
Enchantment cantrip
Casting Time: 1 action
Range: 60 feet
Components: V System
Duration: Instantaneous

You unleash a string of very creative and effective insults at a creature you can see within range. If the target can hear you (though it need not understand you), it must succeed on a Wisdom saving throw or take 1d4 psychic damage and have disadvantage on the next attack roll it makes before the end of its next turn.

This spell's damage increases by 1d4 when you reach 5th level (2d4), 11th level (3d4), and 17th level (4d4).

Level 1

Charm Person
1st-level enchantment
Casting Time: 1 action
Range: 30 feet
Components: V, S
Duration: 1 hour

You attempt to charm a humanoid you can see within range. It must make a Wisdom saving throw, and does so with advantage if you or your companions are fighting it. If it fails the saving throw, it is charmed by you until the spell ends or until you or your companions do anything harmful to it. The charmed creature regards you as a friendly acquaintance. When the spell ends, the creature knows it was charmed by you.

At Higher Levels. When you cast this spell using a spell slot of 2nd level or higher, you can target one additional creature for each slot level above 1st. The creatures must be within 30 feet of each other when you target them.

❁ Disguise Self
1st-level illusion
Casting Time: 1 action
Range: Self
Components: V, S
Duration: 1 hour

You make yourself—including your clothing, armor, weapons, and other belongings on your person—look different until the spell ends or until you use your action to dismiss it. You can seem 1 foot shorter or taller and can appear thin, fat, or in between. You can't change your body type, so you must adopt a form that has the same basic arrangement of limbs. Think of stuffing your shirt with a pillow or wearing a wig.

The changes wrought by this spell fail to hold up to physical inspection. For example, if you use this spell to appear wider than you are, the hand of someone who reaches out to touch you would bump into you and the other person would instantly know that they were touching a pillow and not a person.

To discern that you are disguised, a creature can use its action to inspect your appearance and must succeed on an Intelligence (Investigation) check against your spell save DC.

Hideous Laughter
1st-level enchantment
Casting Time: 1 action
Range: 30 feet
Components: V, S
Duration: Concentration, up to 1 minute

You may cackle in an unsettling way to cause another to feel frightened. The target must succeed on a Wisdom saving throw or fall prone, becoming incapacitated and unable to stand up for the duration. A creature with an Intelligence score of 4 or less isn't affected.

At the end of each of its turns, and each time it takes damage, the target can make another Wisdom saving throw. The target has advantage on the saving throw if it's triggered by damage. On a success, the spell ends.

❖ Sleep
1st-level enchantment
Casting Time: 1 action
Range: 5 feet
Components: V, S
Duration: 1 minute

You use an elaborate knockout move that is 100 percent effective. This spell sends creatures into a slumber. Each creature affected by this spell falls unconscious until the spell ends, the sleeper takes damage, or someone uses an action to shake or slap the sleeper awake.

Because it is a nerve-based knockout, undead aren't affected by this spell.

Level 7

❖ Project Image
7th-level illusion
Casting Time: 1 action
Range: 500 feet
Components: V, S, M (something pertaining to the visual)
Duration: Concentration, up to 1 day

You create an illusory copy of yourself that lasts for the duration. The copy can appear at any location within range that you have seen before, regardless of intervening obstacles. The illusion looks and sounds like you but is intangible. If the illusion takes any damage, it disappears, and the spell ends.

You can use your action to move this illusion up to twice your speed, and make it gesture, speak, and behave in whatever way you choose. It mimics your mannerisms perfectly.

❖ This is an illusion made possible with shadow puppetry, mirror surfaces, or other tangible materials. Materials are required to work the "spell."

Physical interaction with the image reveals it to be an illusion. A creature that uses its action to examine the image can determine that it is an illusion with a successful Intelligence (Investigation) check against your spell save DC. If a creature discerns the illusion for what it is, the creature can see through the image, and any noise it makes sounds hollow to the creature.

Cleric

As a cleric, you gain the following class features.

Hit Points

Hit Dice: 1d8 per cleric level
Hit Points at 1st Level: 8 + your Constitution modifier
Hit Points at Higher Levels: 1d8 (or 5) + your Constitution modifier per cleric level after 1st

Proficiencies

Armor: Light armor, medium armor, shields
Weapons: Simple weapons
Tools: Domain-based
Saving Throws: Wisdom, Charisma
Skills: Choose two from History, Insight, Medicine, Persuasion, and Religion

Equipment

You start with the following equipment, in addition to the equipment granted by your background:

- (a) a mace or (b) a warhammer (if proficient)
- (a) scale mail, (b) leather armor, or (c) chain mail (if proficient)
- (a) a light crossbow and 20 bolts or (b) any simple weapon
- (a) a priest's pack or (b) an explorer's pack
- (a) a shield and a holy symbol

The Cleric

Level	Proficiency Bonus	Features
1	+2	Spells, Divine Domain
2	+2	Spells, Channel Divinity (1/rest), Divine Domain feature
3	+2	Spells
4	+2	Ability Score Improvement
5	+3	Destroy Undead (CR 1/2)
6	+3	Spells, Channel Divinity (2/rest), Divine Domain feature
7	+3	—
8	+3	Ability Score Improvement, Destroy Undead (CR 1), Divine Domain feature
9	+4	—
10	+4	Divine Intervention
11	+4	Destroy Undead (CR 2)
12	+4	Ability Score Improvement
13	+5	—
14	+5	Destroy Undead (CR 3)
15	+5	—
16	+5	Ability Score Improvement
17	+6	Destroy Undead (CR 4), Divine Domain feature
18	+6	Channel Divinity (3/rest)
19	+6	Ability Score Improvement
20	+6	Divine Intervention improvement

Spellcasting

❉ As a conduit for divine power, you can cast cleric spells. For the purpose of Ambergrove in *Ranger's Odyssey*, clerics are mainly cooks and material healers, though they would still have a patron deity for Domain uses.

❉ You know one cantrip and three 1st-level spells from the standard spell list—with modifications—and you will learn three 2nd-level spells, two 3rd-level spells, and one 6th-level spell.

The Cleric table shows how many spell slots you have to cast your spells of 1st level and higher. To cast one of these spells, you must expend a slot of the spell's level or higher. You regain all expended spell slots when you finish a long rest. You prepare the list of cleric spells that are available for you to cast, choosing from the cleric spell list. When you do so, choose a number of cleric spells equal to your Wisdom modifier + your cleric level (minimum of one spell). The spells must be of a level for which you have spell slots. Casting the spell doesn't remove it from your list of prepared spells. You can change your list of prepared spells when you finish a long rest. Preparing a new list of cleric spells requires time spent in prayer and meditation: at least 1 minute per spell level for each spell on your list.

Spellcasting Ability

During the Lost Age, when there is no magic, "cleric spells" refer to personality and food-based nonmagical abilities. Spell restrictions still apply.

Constitution is your spellcasting ability for your cleric spells. The power of your spells comes from your devotion to your deity and your skill with food. You use your Constitution whenever a cleric spell refers to your spellcasting ability. In addition, you use your Constitution modifier when setting the saving throw DC for a cleric spell you cast and when making an attack roll with one.

Spell save DC = 8 + your proficiency bonus + your Constitution modifier

Spell attack modifier = your proficiency bonus + your Constitution modifier

Spellcasting Focus

You can use a holy symbol (see "Equipment") as a spellcasting focus for your cleric spells.

Divine Domain

Choose one domain related to your deity, such as Life. Each domain is detailed at the end of the class description, and each one provides examples of gods associated with it. Your choice grants you domain characteristics and other features when you choose it at 1st level. It also grants you additional ways to use Channel Divinity when you gain that feature at 2nd level, and additional benefits at 6th, 8th, and 17th levels.

Channel Divinity

At 2nd level, you gain the ability to channel divine energy directly from your deity, using that energy to fuel magical effects. You start with two such effects: Turn Undead—*retained as a classic cleric ability despite the no-magic rule*—and an effect determined by your domain. Some domains grant you additional effects as you advance in levels, as noted in the domain description. When you use your Channel Divinity, you choose which effect to create. You must then finish a short or long rest to use your Channel Divinity again. Some Channel Divinity effects require saving throws. When you use such an effect from this class, the DC equals your cleric spell save DC. Beginning at 6th level, you can use your Channel Divinity twice between rests, and beginning at 18th level, you can use it three times between rests. When you finish a short or long rest, you regain your expended uses.

Channel Divinity: Turn Undead

As an action, you present your holy symbol and speak a prayer censuring the undead. Each undead that can see or hear you within 30 feet of you must make a Wisdom saving throw. If the creature fails its saving throw, it is turned for 1 minute or until it takes any damage. A turned creature must spend its turns trying to move as far away from you as it can, and it can't willingly move to a space within 30 feet of you. It also can't take reactions. For its action, it can use only the Dash action or try to escape from an effect that prevents it from moving. If there's nowhere to move, the creature can use the Dodge action.

Ability Score Improvement

When you reach 4th level, and again at 8th, 12th, 16th, and 19th level, you can increase one ability score of your choice by 2, or you can increase two ability scores of your choice by 1. As normal, you can't increase an ability score above 20 using this feature.

Destroy Undead

Starting at 5th level, when an undead fails its saving throw against your Turn Undead feature, the creature is instantly destroyed if its challenge rating is at or below a certain threshold, as shown in the Destroy Undead table.

Cleric Level	Destroys Undead of CR ...
5	1/2 or lower
8	1 or lower
11	2 or lower
14	3 or lower
17	4 or lower

Divine Intervention

Beginning at 10th level, you can call on your deity to intervene on your behalf when your need is great. Imploring your deity's aid requires you to use your action. Describe the assistance you seek, and roll percentile dice. If you roll a number equal to or lower than your cleric level, your deity intervenes. The DM chooses the nature of the intervention; the effect of any cleric spell or cleric domain spell would be appropriate. If your deity intervenes, you can't use this feature again for 7 days. Otherwise, you can use it again after you finish a long rest. At 20th level, your call for intervention succeeds automatically, no roll required.

Life Domain

The Life domain focuses on the vibrant positive energy—one of the fundamental forces of the universe—that sustains all life. The gods of life promote vitality and health through healing the wounded, caring for those in need, and driving away the forces of death and undeath.

Almost any non-evil deity can claim influence over this domain, particularly sun and moon gods (Seaghae and Oaeda), gods of healing or endurance (such as Weanha, Neadae, and Uehrae), and gods of home and community (such as Ean, Gheya, Daeda, and Maonna).

Standard Gear

Life domain clerics have a *healer's kit* among their supplies.

Bonus Proficiency

When you choose this domain at 1st level, you gain proficiency with heavy armor.

Disciple of Life

Also starting at 1st level, your healing spells are more effective. Whenever you use a spell of 1st level or higher to restore hit points to a creature, the creature regains additional hit points equal to 2 + the spell's level.

Channel Divinity: Preserve Life

Starting at 2nd level, you can use your Channel Divinity to heal the badly injured. As an action, you present your holy symbol and evoke healing energy that can restore a number of hit points equal to five times your cleric level. Choose any creatures within 30 feet of you, and divide those hit points among them. This feature can restore a creature to no more than half of its hit point maximum. You can't use this feature on an undead or a construct.

Blessed Healer

Beginning at 6th level, the healing spells you cast on others heal you as well. When you cast a spell of 1st level or higher that restores hit points to a creature other than you, you regain hit points equal to 2 + the spell's level.

Divine Strike

At 8th level, you gain the ability to infuse your weapon strikes with divine energy. Once on each of your turns when you hit a creature with a weapon attack, you can cause the attack to deal an extra 1d8 radiant damage to the target. When you reach 14th level, the extra damage increases to 2d8.

Supreme Healing

Starting at 17th level, when you would normally roll one or more dice to restore hit points with a spell, you instead use the highest number possible for each die. For example, instead of restoring 2d6 hit points to a creature, you restore 12.

Death Domain

The Death domain focuses on the corruptive negative energy that damages all life. The gods of darkness promote decay and death through injury to others and twisted uses of the clerical "magic."

Aside from the goddess of death, Easha, who is herself not evil, combat deities (such as Taerg), and the trickster (Paeor), this domain is chiefly influenced by the two dark deities of Ambergrove—Haeyla and Toren.

Bonus Proficiency

When you choose this domain at 1st level, you gain an additional proficiency with simple weapons.

Twisted Magic

As a follower of a twisted domain, your magic is still restricted to the few approved spells. However, they have the opposite effect to the intended. Instead of *aid* helping the target, it weakens the target. Instead of *beacon of hope* bestowing hope and vitality, it instead causes fear and frailty.

> Refer to the **Twisted** description under each spell.

Disciple of Death

Also starting at 1st level, your twisted healing spells are more effective. Whenever you use a spell of 1st level or higher to take hit points from a creature, the creature loses additional hit points equal to 2 + the spell's level.

Channel Divinity: Extinguish Life

Starting at 2nd level, you can use your Channel Divinity to badly injure an uninjured enemy before an encounter. As an action, you present your holy symbol and evoke twisted healing energy that can remove a number of hit points equal to five times your cleric level. Choose any creatures within 30 feet of you, and divide those hit points among them. This feature can injure a creature to no less than half of its hit point maximum. You can't use this feature on an undead or a construct.

Cursed Healer

Beginning at 6th level, the twisted healing spells you cast on others *heal* you as well. When you cast a spell of 1st level or higher that restores hit points to a creature other than you (before it is twisted), you regain hit points equal to 2 + the spell's level.

Divine Strike

At 8th level, you gain the ability to infuse your weapon strikes with divine energy. Once on each of your turns when you hit a creature with a weapon attack, you can cause the attack to deal an extra 1d8 radiant damage to the target. When you reach 14th level, the extra damage increases to 2d8.

Supreme Harming

Starting at 17th level, when you would normally roll one or more dice to take hit points with a spell, you instead use the highest number possible for each die. For example, instead of taking 2d6 hit points from a creature, you take 12.

Feast Domain

The Feast domain focuses on the experienced use of food to help others, either in standard or emotional healing or to fill the belly. The gods of sustenance promote vitality and health through healing the sick, caring for those in need, and curing poisons and diseases.

Almost any non-evil deity can claim influence over this domain, particularly agricultural deities (such as Aeun, Eaogh, and Ghehr), gods of healing or endurance (such as Weanha, Neadae, and Uehrae), and gods of home and community (such as Ean, Gheya, Daeda, and Maonna).

Standard Gear

Feast domain clerics have *cook's utensils* among their supplies.

Bonus Proficiency

When you choose this domain at 1st level, you gain proficiency with heavy armor.

Disciple of the Feast

Also starting at 1st level, your food and drink spells are more effective. Whenever you use a spell of 1st level or higher to create or purify food, 2 + the spell's level is added to the effect radius.

Channel Divinity: Favored Foodstuffs

Starting at 2nd level, you can use your Channel Divinity to provide one chosen food or drink item to an ally. As an action, you present your holy symbol and evoke sustaining energy that conjures food or drink for a maximum of 5 creatures (+ 1 per cleric level) for 1 hour.

Blessed Cook

Beginning at 6th level, the food-based spells you cast heal you as well. When you cast a spell of 1st level or higher that grants consumables to another, you regain hit points equal to the spell's level. For example, if you use *create food and water,* a 3rd-level spell, you gain three hit points up to your maximum.

Divine Strike

At 8th level, you gain the ability to infuse your weapon strikes with divine energy. Once on each of your turns when you hit a creature with a weapon attack, you can cause the attack to deal an extra 1d8 radiant damage to the target. When you reach 14th level, the extra damage increases to 2d8.

Supreme Restoration

Starting at 17th level, when affected players would normally roll one or more dice to apply the positive effects of *heroes' feast,* they instead apply a set number. The player's hit point maximum increases by 20. In addition, players will be able to roll 4d10 total in the 24-hour benefit period to regain hit points.

Botulism Domain

Botulin is a toxin typically present in spoiled, fermented, or improperly canned foods on Earth. The Botulism domain focuses on the experienced use of food to harm another either by poisoning or the transmission of disease, destroying from the inside. The gods of decay promote sickness by twisting food and drink.

Aside from the goddess of death, Easha, and powers twisted from the agricultural deities (such as Aeun, Eaogh, and Ghehr) and the goddess of healing (Weanha), this domain is chiefly influenced by the two dark deities of Ambergrove—Haeyla and Toren.

Standard Gear

Botulism domain clerics have *poisoner's tools* among their supplies.

Bonus Proficiency

When you choose this domain at 1st level, you gain an additional proficiency with simple weapons.

Twisted Magic

As a follower of a twisted domain, your magic is still restricted to the few approved spells. However, they have the opposite effect to the intended. Instead of *detect poison and disease* revealing dangers, it hides them. *Purify food and drink* makes the consumable impure, and *create food and water* decays existing sustenance or creates food and water that is inedible.

Refer to the **Twisted** description under each spell.

Disciple of the Feast

Also starting at 1st level, your twisted food and drink spells are more effective. Whenever you use a spell of 1st level or higher to decay or impurify food, 2 + the spell's level is added to the effect radius.

Channel Divinity: Sullied Slop

Starting at 2nd level, you can use your Channel Divinity to provide one chosen twisted food or drink item to an enemy. As an action, you present your holy symbol and evoke corrupting energy that conjures food or drink for a maximum of 5 creatures (+ 1 per cleric level) for 1 hour. After an hour, your enemies will realize that they have been consuming twisted goods.

Blessed Cook

Beginning at 6th level, the food-based spells you cast *heal* you. When you cast a spell of 1st level or higher that grants twisted consumables to another, you regain hit points equal to the spell's level. For example, if you use *create food and water,* a 3rd-level spell, you gain three hit points up to your maximum. Even though you are using twisted magic, you gain healing with this feature.

Divine Strike

At 8th level, you gain the ability to infuse your weapon strikes with divine energy. Once on each of your turns when you hit a creature with a weapon attack, you can cause the attack to deal an extra 1d8 radiant damage to the target. When you reach 14th level, the extra damage increases to 2d8.

Supreme Corruption

Starting at 17th level, when affected enemies would normally roll one or more dice to apply the negative effects of twisted *heroes' feast,* they instead apply a set number. The player's hit point maximum decreases by up to 20. In addition, the Botulist cleric will be able to roll up to 1d10 per enemy affected by *heroes' feast* to inflict food poisoning damage during a triggered encounter.

Restricted Spellbook

Cantrips

Mending

Transmutation cantrip

Casting Time: 1 minute

Range: Touch

Components: V, S, M (needle and thread)

Duration: Instantaneous

This spell repairs a single break or tear in an object you touch, such as a broken chain link, two halves of a broken key, a torn cloak, or a leaking wineskin. As long as the break or tear is no larger than 1 foot in any dimension, you mend it, leaving no trace of the former damage.

This spell can physically repair a magic item or construct, but the spell can't restore magic to such an object.

This is really just extremely skilled mending, like that of a grandmother seamstress.

Twisted Instead of mending the item, it is torn or otherwise broken.

Level 1

Cure Wounds

1st-level evocation

Casting Time: 1 action

Range: Touch

Components: V, S; M (a bandage of any size)

Duration: Instantaneous

A creature you touch regains a number of hit points equal to 1d8 + your spellcasting ability modifier. This spell has no effect on undead or constructs.

You use advanced medical knowledge to dress wounds, coming from training by an Earther.

At Higher Levels. When you cast this spell using a spell slot of 2nd level or higher, the healing increases by 1d8 for each slot level above 1st.

Twisted instead of gaining hit points, the creature loses hit points.

Detect Poison and Disease

1st-level divination (ritual)

Casting Time: 1 action

Range: Self

Components: V, S, M (a spoon)

Duration: Concentration, up to 10 minutes

For the duration, you can sense the presence and location of poisons, poisonous creatures, and diseases within 30 feet of you. You also identify the kind of poison, poisonous creature, or disease in each case.

You use your knowledge of food and plants to identify potential hazards.

The spell can penetrate most barriers, but it is blocked by 1 foot of stone, 1 inch of common metal, a thin sheet of lead, or 3 feet of wood or dirt.

Twisted Instead of detecting ill effects, you are able to conceal them from others.

Purify Food and Drink

1st-level transmutation (ritual)

Casting Time: 1 action

Range: 10 feet

Components: V, S, M (spices)

Duration: Instantaneous

All nonmagical food and drink within a 5-foot-radius sphere centered on a point of your choice within range is purified and rendered free of poison and disease.

Twisted All food and drink within a 5-foot-radius is completely contaminated by a poison, disease, or disgusting insect.

LEVEL 2

Aid
2nd-level abjuration
Casting Time: 1 action
Range: 30 feet
Components: V, S, M (white cloth or a cookie, depending on domain)
Duration: 8 hours

Your spell bolsters your allies with toughness and resolve. Choose up to three creatures within range. Each target's hit point maximum and current hit points increase by 5 for the duration.

At Higher Levels. When you cast this spell using a spell slot of 3rd level or higher, a target's hit points increase by an additional 5 for each slot level above 2nd.

Twisted Your spell weakens your enemies. Choose up to three targets. Each target's hit point maximum and current hit points decrease by 5 for the duration. For each level above 2nd, these decrease by an additional 2.

Calm Emotions
2nd-level enchantment
Casting Time: 1 action
Range: 60 feet
Components: V, S
Duration: Concentration, up to 1 minute

You attempt to suppress strong emotions in a group of people. Each humanoid in a 20-foot-radius sphere centered on a point you choose within range must make a Charisma saving throw; a creature can choose to fail this saving throw if it wishes. If a creature fails its saving throw, choose one of the following two effects.

You can suppress any effect causing a target to be charmed or frightened. When this spell ends, any suppressed effect resumes, provided that its duration has not expired in the meantime.

Alternatively, you can make a target indifferent about creatures of your choice that it is hostile toward. This indifference ends if the target is attacked or harmed by a spell or if it witnesses any of its friends being harmed. When the spell ends, the creature becomes hostile again, unless the DM rules otherwise.

You use your own kindness and care to convince them instead of magic.

Twisted Instead of calming emotions, you make your target nervous or afraid.

Prayer of Healing
2nd-level evocation
Casting Time: 10 minutes
Range: 30 feet
Components: V
Duration: Instantaneous

Up to six creatures of your choice that you can see within range each regain hit points equal to 2d8 + your spellcasting ability modifier. This spell has no effect on undead or constructs.

Your will is strong enough to send positive thoughts that heal.

At Higher Levels. When you cast this spell using a spell slot of 3rd level or higher, the healing increases by 1d8 for each slot level above 2nd.

Twisted This becomes a curse of injury that causes up to three different creatures to lose hit points equal to 2d8. For every even level beginning with 4th, the damage increases by 1d8.

Level 3

<u>Beacon of Hope</u>

3rd-level abjuration

Casting Time: 1 action

Range: 30 feet

Components: V, S

Duration: Concentration, up to 1 minute

❁ This spell bestows hope and vitality. Choose any number of creatures within range. For the duration, each target has advantage on Constitution saving throws and death saving throws, and regains the maximum number of hit points possible from any healing.

❁ **Twisted** For the duration, each target has disadvantage on Constitution saving throws and death saving throws and regains the minimum number of hit points possible from any healing.

<u>Create Food and Water</u>

3rd-level conjuration

Casting Time: 1 action

Range: 30 feet

Components: V, S

Duration: Instantaneous

You create 45 pounds of food and 30 gallons of water on the ground or in containers within range, enough to sustain up to fifteen humanoids or five steeds for 24 hours. The food is bland but nourishing, and spoils if uneaten after 24 hours. The water is clean and doesn't go bad.

❁ This is possible thanks to your superior cooking skills.

❁ **Twisted** You create the same amount of food, but it is all contaminated. It looks and tastes fine, but the water is filled with parasites and the food is maggoty. Alternately, you can contaminate existing food. After 2 hours, if those who ate the food are still alive, they must pass a Constitution saving throw with disadvantage.

Level 6

<u>Heroes' Feast</u>

6th-level conjuration

Casting Time: 10 minutes

Range: 30 feet

❁ **Components:** V, S, M (a gem-encrusted bowl worth at least 500 gp, which the spell consumes)

Duration: Instantaneous

You bring forth a great feast, including magnificent food and drink. The feast takes 1 hour to consume and disappears at the end of that time, and the beneficial effects don't set in until this hour is over. Up to twelve other creatures can partake of the feast.

A creature that partakes of the feast gains several benefits. The creature is cured of all diseases and poison, becomes immune to poison and being frightened, and makes all Wisdom and Constitution saving throws with advantage. Its hit point maximum also increases by 2d10, and it gains the same number of hit points. These benefits last for 24 hours.

❁ **Twisted** You create the same amount of food, but it is all contaminated. It looks and tastes fine, but the water is filled with parasites and the food is maggoty. A creature that partakes of the feast faces several hardships. The creature becomes poisoned and frightened and makes all Wisdom and Constitution saving throws with disadvantage. Its hit point maximum decreases by 2d10 and it loses 1d10 number of hit points. These effects last for 24 hours.

Fighter

As a fighter, you gain the following class features.

Hit Points

Hit Dice: 1d10 per fighter level
Hit Points at 1st Level: 10 + your Constitution modifier
Hit Points at Higher Levels: 1d10 (or 6) + your Constitution modifier per fighter level after 1st

Proficiencies

Armor: All armor, shields
Weapons: Simple weapons, martial weapons
Tools: None
Saving Throws: Strength, Constitution
Skills: Choose two skills from Acrobatics, Animal Handling, Athletics, History, Insight, Intimidation, Perception, and Survival

Equipment

You start with the following equipment, in addition to the equipment granted by your background:

- (a) chain mail or (b) leather armor, longbow, and 20 arrows
- (a) a martial weapon and a shield or (b) two martial weapons
- (a) a light crossbow and 20 bolts or (b) two handaxes
- (a) a dungeoneer's pack or (b) an explorer's pack

The Fighter

Level	Proficiency Bonus	Feature
1	+2	Fighting Style, Second Wind
2	+2	Action Surge (one use)
3	+2	Martial Archetype
4	+2	Ability Score Improvement
5	+3	Extra Attack
6	+3	Ability Score Improvement
7	+3	Martial Archetype feature
8	+3	Ability Score Improvement
9	+4	Indomitable (one use)
10	+4	Martial Archetype feature
11	+4	Extra Attack (2)
12	+4	Ability Score Improvement
13	+5	Indomitable (two uses)
14	+5	Ability Score Improvement
15	+5	Martial Archetype feature
16	+5	Ability Score Improvement
17	+6	Action Surge (two uses), Indomitable (three uses)
18	+6	Martial Archetype feature
19	+6	Ability Score Improvement
20	+6	Extra Attack (3)

Fighting Style

You adopt a particular style of fighting as your specialty. Choose one of the following options. You can't take a Fighting Style option more than once, even if you later get to choose again.

Archery

You gain a +2 bonus to attack rolls you make with ranged weapons.

Defense

While you are wearing armor, you gain a +1 bonus to AC.

Dueling

When you are wielding a melee weapon in one hand and no other weapons, you gain a +2 bonus to damage rolls with that weapon.

Great Weapon Fighting

When you roll a 1 or 2 on a damage die for an attack you make with a melee weapon that you are wielding with two hands, you can reroll the die and must use the new roll, even if the new roll is a 1 or a 2. The weapon must have the two-handed or versatile property for you to gain this benefit.

Protection

When a creature you can see attacks a target other than you that is within 5 feet of you, you can use your reaction to impose disadvantage on the attack roll. You must be wielding a shield.

Two-Weapon Fighting

When you engage in two-weapon fighting, you can add your ability modifier to the damage of the second attack.

Second Wind

You have a limited well of stamina that you can draw on to protect yourself from harm. On your turn, you can use a bonus action to regain hit points equal to 1d10 + your fighter level. Once you use this feature, you must finish a short or long rest before you can use it again.

Action Surge

Starting at 2nd level, you can push yourself beyond your normal limits for a moment. On your turn, you can take one additional action on top of your regular action and a possible bonus action.

Once you use this feature, you must finish a short or long rest before you can use it again. Starting at 17th level, you can use it twice before a rest, but only once on the same turn.

Martial Archetype

At 3rd level, you choose an archetype that you strive to emulate in your combat styles and techniques, such as Champion. The archetype you choose grants you features at 3rd level and again at 7th, 10th, 15th, and 18th level.

> The level-based archetype benefits are identical between the archetypes. The advantage and approach are the only differences.

Improved Critical

Beginning when you choose this archetype at 3rd level, your weapon attacks score a critical hit on a roll of 19 or 20.

Remarkable Athlete

Starting at 7th level, you can add half your proficiency bonus (round up) to any Strength, Dexterity, or Constitution check you make that doesn't already use your proficiency bonus.

In addition, when you make a running long jump, the distance you can cover increases by a number of feet equal to your Strength modifier.

Additional Fighting Style

At 10th level, you can choose a second option from the Fighting Style class feature.

Superior Critical

Starting at 15th level, your weapon attacks score a critical hit on a roll of 18–20.

Survivor

At 18th level, you attain the pinnacle of resilience in battle. At the start of each of your turns, you regain hit points equal to 5 + your Constitution modifier if you have no more than half of your hit points left. You don't gain this benefit if you have 0 hit points.

Ability Score Improvement

When you reach 4th level, and again at 6th, 8th, 12th, 14th, 16th, and 19th level, you can increase one ability score of your choice by 2, or you can increase two ability scores of your choice by 1. As normal, you can't increase an ability score above 20 using this feature.

Extra Attack

Beginning at 5th level, you can attack twice, instead of once, whenever you take the Attack action on your turn.

The number of attacks increases to three when you reach 11th level in this class and to four when you reach 20th level in this class.

Indomitable

Beginning at 9th level, you can reroll a saving throw that you fail. If you do so, you must use the new roll, and you can't use this feature again until you finish a long rest.

You can use this feature twice between long rests starting at 13th level and three times between long rests starting at 17th level.

Martial Archetypes

Different fighters choose different approaches to perfecting their fighting prowess. The martial archetype you choose to emulate reflects your approach.

Champion

The archetypal Champion focuses on the development of raw physical power honed to deadly perfection. Those who model themselves on this archetype combine rigorous training with physical excellence to deal devastating blows.

The champion gains an advantage when fighting one or two enemies.

Defender

The archetypal Defender focuses on using their own strength to protect others rather than to enforce their own will. The defender gains an advantage when in front of someone else.

Finesser

The archetypal Finesser uses others' size against them, focusing on agility to defeat enemies rather than force. The finesser gains advantage when fighting someone of larger size or lower intelligence.

Naadakh

As a naadakh, you gain the following class features. This class is derived from the monk class, so the ❁ indicator appears when something differs from the monk class other than the name.

❁ As mentioned in the Human race information, the human cultures in Ambergrove are derived from a variety of ancient Earth cultures. This one comes from Mongolia. As with other aspects between Ambergrove and Earth, this is distorted from the original source. Please research *Mongolian wrestling, Naadam, Naadakh,* and *Bökh* for real-life information about this storied culture.

Hit Points

Hit Dice: 1d8 per naadakh level
Hit Points at 1st Level: 8 + your Constitution modifier
Hit Points at Higher Levels: 1d8 (or 5) + your Constitution modifier per monk level after 1st

Proficiencies

Armor: None
Weapons: Simple weapons, shortswords
Tools: Choose one type of artisan's tools or one musical instrument
Saving Throws: Strength, Dexterity Skills: Choose two from Acrobatics, Athletics, History, Insight, Religion, and Stealth

Equipment

You start with the following equipment, in addition to the equipment granted by your background:

- (a) a shortsword or (b) any simple weapon
- (a) a dungeoneer's pack or (b) an explorer's pack
- (a) 10 darts

The Naadakh

Level	Proficiency Bonus	Martial Arts	Qi Points	Unarmored Movement	Features
1	+2	1d4	—	—	Unarmored Defense, Bökh
2	+2	1d4	2	+10 ft.	Qi, Unarmored Movement
3	+2	1d4	3	+10 ft.	Naadam, Deflect Missiles
4	+2	1d4	4	+10 ft.	Ability Score Improvement, Slow Fall
5	+3	1d6	5	+10 ft.	Extra Attack, Stunning Strike
6	+3	1d6	6	+15 ft.	Qi-Empowered Strikes, Naadam feature
7	+3	1d6	7	+15 ft.	Evasion, Stillness of Mind
8	+3	1d6	8	+15 ft.	Ability Score Improvement
9	+4	1d6	9	+15 ft.	Unarmored Movement improvement
10	+4	1d6	10	+20 ft.	Purity of Body
11	+4	1d8	11	+20 ft.	Naadam feature
12	+4	1d8	12	+20 ft.	Ability Score Improvement
13	+5	1d8	13	+20 ft.	Tongue of the Sun and Moon
14	+5	1d8	14	+25 ft.	Diamond Soul
15	+5	1d8	15	+25 ft.	Timeless Body
16	+5	1d8	16	+25 ft.	Ability Score Improvement
17	+6	1d10	17	+25 ft.	Naadam feature
18	+6	1d10	18	+30 ft.	Empty Body

19	+6	1d10	19	+30 ft.	Ability Score Improvement
20	+6	1d10	20	+30 ft.	Perfect Self

Unarmored Defense

Beginning at 1st level, while you are wearing no armor and not wielding a shield, your AC equals 10 + your Dexterity modifier + your Wisdom modifier.

Bökh

At 1st level, your practice of bökh gives you mastery of combat styles that use unarmed strikes and naadakh weapons, which are shortswords and any simple melee weapons that don't have the two-handed or heavy property.

You gain the following benefits while you are unarmed or wielding only naadakh weapons and you aren't wearing armor or wielding a shield:

- You can use Dexterity instead of Strength for the attack and damage rolls of your unarmed strikes and naadakh weapons.
- You can roll a d4 in place of the normal damage of your unarmed strike or naadakh weapon. This die changes as you gain naadakh levels, as shown in the Martial Arts column of the Naadakh table.
- When you use the Attack action with an unarmed strike or a naadakh weapon on your turn, you can make one unarmed strike as a bonus action. For example, if you take the Attack action and attack with a quarterstaff, you can also make an unarmed strike as a bonus action, assuming you haven't already taken a bonus action this turn.

Some bökh fighters use specialized forms of the naadakh weapons. Weapon choices should all be small finesse weapons. Whatever name you use for a naadakh weapon, you can use the game statistics provided for the weapon.

Qi

Starting at 2nd level, your training allows you to harness the mystic energy of qi. Your access to this energy is represented by a number of qi points. Your naadakh level determines the number of points you have, as shown in the Qi Points column of the Naadakh table.

You can spend these points to fuel various qi features. You start knowing three such features: Flurry of Blows, Patient Defense, and Step of the Wind. You learn more qi features as you gain levels in this class.

When you spend a qi point, it is unavailable until you finish a short or long rest, at the end of which you draw all of your expended qi back into yourself. You must spend at least 30 minutes of the rest meditating to regain your qi points.

Some of your qi features require your target to make a saving throw to resist the feature's effects. The saving throw DC is calculated as follows:

Qi save DC = 8 + your proficiency bonus + your Wisdom modifier

Qi is the Mongolian word for *chi*.

Flurry of Blows

Immediately after you take the Attack action on your turn, you can spend 1 qi point to make two unarmed strikes as a bonus action.

Patient Defense

You can spend 1 qi point to take the Dodge action as a bonus action on your turn.

Step of the Wind

You can spend 1 qi point to take the Disengage or Dash action as a bonus action on your turn, and your jump distance is doubled for the turn.

Unarmored Movement

Starting at 2nd level, your speed increases by 10 feet while you are not wearing armor or wielding a shield. This bonus increases when you reach certain naadakh levels, as shown in the Naadakh table.

At 9th level, you gain the ability to move along vertical surfaces and across liquids on your turn without falling during the move.

Naadam

When you reach 3rd level, you begin earning titles as set in the Naadam—a yearly Mongolian festival competition that awards status to bökh fighters who win rounds. Your status grants you features at 3rd level and again at 6th, 11th, and 17th level, as well as titles at various levels.

Deflect Missiles

Starting at 3rd level, you can use your reaction to deflect or catch the missile when you are hit by a ranged weapon attack. When you do so, the damage you take from the attack is reduced by 1d10 + your Dexterity modifier + your naadakh level.

If you reduce the damage to 0, you can catch the missile if it is small enough for you to hold in one hand and you have at least one hand free. If you catch a missile in this way, you can spend 1 qi point to make a ranged attack with the weapon or piece of ammunition you just caught, as part of the same reaction. You make this attack with proficiency, regardless of your weapon proficiencies, and the missile counts as a naadakh weapon for the attack, which has a normal range of 20 feet and a long range of 60 feet.

Ability Score Improvement

When you reach 4th level, and again at 8th, 12th, 16th, and 19th level, you can increase one ability score of your choice by 2, or you can increase two ability scores of your choice by 1. As normal, you can't increase an ability score above 20 using this feature.

Slow Fall

Beginning at 4th level, you can use your reaction when you fall to reduce any falling damage you take by an amount equal to five times your naadakh level.

Extra Attack

Beginning at 5th level, you can attack twice, instead of once, whenever you take the Attack action on your turn.

Stunning Strike

Starting at 5th level, you can interfere with the flow of qi in an opponent's body. When you hit another creature with a melee weapon attack, you can spend 1 qi point to attempt a stunning strike. The target must succeed on a Constitution saving throw or be stunned until the end of your next turn.

Qi-Empowered Strikes

Starting at 6th level, your unarmed strikes count as qi for the purpose of overcoming resistance and immunity to nonmagical attacks and damage.

Evasion

At 7th level, your instinctive agility lets you dodge out of the way of certain area effects. When you are subjected to an effect that allows you to make a Dexterity saving throw to take only half damage, you instead take no damage if you succeed on the saving throw, and only half damage if you fail.

Stillness of Mind

Starting at 7th level, you can use your action to end one effect on yourself that is causing you to be charmed or frightened.

Purity of Body

At 10th level, your mastery of the qi flowing through you makes you immune to disease and poison.

Tongue of the Sun and Moon

Starting at 13th level, you learn to touch the qi of other minds so that you understand all spoken languages. Moreover, any creature that can understand a language can understand what you say.

Diamond Soul

Beginning at 14th level, your mastery of qi grants you proficiency in all saving throws.

Additionally, whenever you make a saving throw and fail, you can spend 1 qi point to reroll it and take the second result.

Timeless Body

At 15th level, your qi sustains you so that you suffer none of the frailty of old age, and you can't be aged magically. You can still die of old age, however. In addition, you no longer need food or water.

Empty Body

Beginning at 18th level, you can use your action to spend 4 qi points to become invisible for 1 minute. During that time, you also have resistance to all damage but force damage.

Additionally, you can spend 8 qi points to cast the astral projection spell, without needing material components. When you do so, you can't take any other creatures with you.

Perfect Self

At 20th level, when you roll for initiative and have no qi points remaining, you regain 4 qi points.

Naadam

Naadakhs are the ultimate masters of martial arts combat, whether armed or unarmed. They learn techniques to push and trip their opponents, manipulate qi to heal damage to their bodies, and practice advanced meditation that can protect them from harm.

❁ As part of the Naadam, accomplished naadakhs prove themselves as masters of their order and earn a title. At certain levels, you earn a higher status title as a naadakh based on your prowess with bökh fighting.

Level	Title
3	Viper
5	Falcon
6	Hawk
7	Elephant
9	Lion
11	Titan
17	Choice from: *Takhi, Khiimori,* or Wind Horse

❁ Practiced Technique

Starting at 3rd level, you can manipulate your enemy's qi when you harness your own. Whenever you hit a creature with one of the attacks granted by your Flurry of Blows, you can impose one of the following effects on that target:

- It must succeed on a Dexterity saving throw or be knocked prone.
- It must make a Strength saving throw. If it fails, you can push it up to 15 feet away from you.
- It can't take reactions until the end of your next turn.

Wholeness of Body

At 6th level, you gain the ability to heal yourself. As an action, you can regain hit points equal to three times your naadakh level. You must finish a long rest before you can use this feature again.

Tranquility

Beginning at 11th level, you can enter a special meditation that surrounds you with an aura of peace. At the end of a long rest, you gain the effect of a sanctuary spell that lasts until the start of your next long rest (the spell can end early as normal). The saving throw DC for the spell equals 8 + your Wisdom modifier + your proficiency bonus.

Quivering Palm

At 17th level, you gain the ability to set up lethal vibrations in someone's body. When you hit a creature with an unarmed strike, you can spend 3 qi points to start these imperceptible vibrations, which last for a number of days equal to your naadakh level. The vibrations are harmless unless you use your action to end them. To do so, you and the target must be on the same plane of existence. When you use this action, the creature must make a Constitution saving throw. If it fails, it is reduced to 0 hit points. If it succeeds, it takes 10d10 necrotic damage.

You can have only one creature under the effect of this feature at a time. You can choose to end the vibrations harmlessly without using an action.

Paladin

As a paladin, you gain the following class features.

Hit Points

Hit Dice: 1d10 per paladin level
Hit Points at 1st Level: 10 + your Constitution modifier
Hit Points at Higher Levels: 1d10 (or 6) + your Constitution modifier per paladin level after 1st

Proficiencies

Armor: All armor, shields
Weapons: Simple weapons, martial weapons
Tools: None
Saving Throws: Wisdom, Charisma
Skills: Choose two from Athletics, Insight, Intimidation, Medicine, Persuasion, and Religion

Equipment

You start with the following equipment, in addition to the equipment granted by your background:

- (a) a martial weapon and a shield or (b) two martial weapons
- (a) five javelins or (b) any simple melee weapon
- (a) a priest's pack or (b) an explorer's pack
- (a) chain mail and a holy symbol

The Paladin

Level	Proficiency Bonus	Features
1	+2	Divine Sense, Lay on Hands
2	+2	Fighting Style, Spellcasting, Divine Smite
3	+2	Divine Health, Sacred Oath, Channel Divinity
4	+2	Ability Score Improvement
5	+3	Extra Attack
6	+3	Aura of Protection

7	+3	Sacred Oath feature
8	+3	Ability Score Improvement
9	+4	—
10	+4	Aura of Courage
11	+4	Improved Divine Smite
12	+4	Ability Score Improvement
13	+5	—
14	+5	Cleansing Touch
15	+5	Sacred Oath feature
16	+5	Ability Score Improvement
17	+6	—
18	+6	Aura improvements
19	+6	Ability Score Improvement
20	+6	Sacred Oath feature

Divine Sense

The presence of strong evil registers on your senses like a noxious odor, and powerful good rings like heavenly music in your ears. As an action, you can open your awareness to detect such forces. Until the end of your next turn, you know the location of any gods or evil beings within 60 feet of you that is not behind total cover. You know the type of any being whose presence you sense, but not its identity. Within the same radius, you also detect the presence of any place or object that has been consecrated or desecrated, as with the hallow spell.

You can use this feature a number of times equal to 1 + your Charisma modifier. When you finish a long rest, you regain all expended uses.

Lay on Hands

Your blessed touch can heal wounds. You have a pool of healing power that replenishes when you take a long rest. With that pool, you can restore a total number of hit points equal to your paladin level × 5.

As an action, you can touch a creature and draw power from the pool to restore a number of hit points to that creature, up to the maximum amount remaining in your pool.

Alternatively, you can expend 5 hit points from your pool of healing to cure the target of one disease or neutralize one poison affecting it. You can cure multiple diseases and neutralize multiple poisons with a single use of Lay on Hands, expending hit points separately for each one.

This feature has no effect on undead and constructs.

Fighting Style

At 2nd level, you adopt a style of fighting as your specialty. Choose one of the following options. You can't take a Fighting Style option more than once, even if you later get to choose again.

Defense

While you are wearing armor, you gain a +1 bonus to AC.

Dueling

When you are wielding a melee weapon in one hand and no other weapons, you gain a +2 bonus to damage rolls with that weapon.

Great Weapon Fighting

When you roll a 1 or 2 on a damage die for an attack you make with a melee weapon that you are wielding with two hands, you can reroll the die and must use the new roll. The weapon must have the two-handed or versatile property for you to gain this benefit.

Protection

When a creature you can see attacks a target other than you that is within 5 feet of you, you can use your reaction to impose disadvantage on the attack roll. You must be wielding a shield.

❖ Spellcasting

By 2nd level, you have learned to draw on divine magic through meditation and prayer to cast spells as a cleric does. However, you can *only* use *cure light wounds*. No other spells are permitted for the paladin.

Charisma is your spellcasting ability for your *cure light wounds*, since your power derives from the strength of your convictions.

You can use a holy symbol as a spellcasting focus for your paladin spells.

❖ Divine Smite

Starting at 2nd level, when you hit a creature with a melee weapon attack, you can deal radiant damage to the target once per day, in addition to the weapon's damage. The extra damage is 2d8 at 1st level, plus 1d8 for each odd level higher than 1st, to a maximum of 5d8. The damage increases by 1d8 if the target is an undead or a fiend.

Divine Health

By 3rd level, the divine essence flowing through you makes you immune to disease.

Channel Divinity

Your oath allows you to channel divine energy to fuel magical effects. Each Channel Divinity option provided by your oath explains how to use it.

When you use your Channel Divinity, you choose which option to use. You must then finish a short or long rest to use your Channel Divinity again.

Some Channel Divinity effects require saving throws. When you use such an effect from this class, the DC equals your paladin spell save DC.

Ability Score Improvement

When you reach 4th level, and again at 8th, 12th, 16th, and 19th level, you can increase one ability score of your choice by 2, or you can increase two ability scores of your choice by 1. As normal, you can't increase an ability score above 20 using this feature.

Extra Attack

Beginning at 5th level, you can attack twice, instead of once, whenever you take the Attack action on your turn.

Aura of Protection

Starting at 6th level, whenever you or a friendly creature within 10 feet of you must make a saving throw, the creature gains a bonus to the saving throw equal to your Charisma modifier (with a minimum bonus of +1). You must be conscious to grant this bonus.

At 18th level, the range of this aura increases to 30 feet.

Aura of Courage

Starting at 10th level, you and friendly creatures within 10 feet of you can't be frightened while you are conscious.

At 18th level, the range of this aura increases to 30 feet.

Improved Divine Smite

By 11th level, you are so suffused with righteous might that all your melee weapon strikes carry divine power with them. Whenever you hit a creature with a melee weapon, the creature takes an extra 1d8 radiant damage. If you also use your Divine Smite with an attack, you add this damage to the extra damage of your Divine Smite.

Cleansing Touch

Beginning at 14th level, you can use your action to end one negative effect on yourself or on one willing creature that you touch.

You can use this feature a number of times equal to your Charisma modifier (a minimum of once). You regain expended uses when you finish a long rest.

Sacred Oaths

Becoming a paladin involves taking vows that commit the paladin to the cause of righteousness, an active path of fighting wickedness. The final oath, taken when he or she reaches 3rd level, is the culmination of all the paladin's training. Some characters with this class don't consider themselves true paladins until they have reached 3rd level and made this oath. For others, the actual swearing of the oath is a formality, an official stamp on what has always been true in the paladin's heart.

Oath of Devotion

The Oath of Devotion binds a paladin to the loftiest ideals of justice, virtue, and order. Sometimes called cavaliers, white knights, or holy warriors, these paladins meet the ideal of the knight in shining armor, acting with honor in pursuit of justice and the greater good. They hold themselves to the highest standards of conduct, and some, for better or worse, hold the rest of the world to the same standards. Many who swear this oath are devoted to gods of law and good and use their gods' tenets as the measure of their devotion.

Tenets of Devotion

Though the exact words and strictures of the Oath of Devotion vary, paladins of this oath share these tenets.

Honesty. Don't lie or cheat. Let your word be your promise.

Courage. Never fear to act, though caution is wise.

Compassion. Aid others, protect the weak, and punish those who threaten them. Show mercy to your foes, but temper it with wisdom.

Honor. Treat others with fairness, and let your honorable deeds be an example to them. Do as much good as possible while causing the least amount of harm.

Duty. Be responsible for your actions and their consequences, protect those entrusted to your care, and obey those who have just authority over you.

> Because this is a time without magic, standard paladin benefits from oaths would not apply. This being the case, the path at this time has been simplified. As an Ambergrove paladin, you must be good and hold yourself to the betterment of others. However, you may have a wide range of devotees—chosen focus of your devotion.

Devotee

There is no boundary to your devotee unless set by your DM. Your only limit is your imagination. Choose anything that your character would feel strongly enough toward to protect at all costs. Think of it like being the patron saint of something.

A few ideas:

- Nature
- Sailing
- Warriors
- Kindness

- Light
- Warmth

Channel Divinity

When you take this oath at 3rd level, you gain the following two Channel Divinity options.

Sacred Weapon. As an action, you can imbue one weapon that you are holding with positive energy, using your Channel Divinity. For 1 minute, you add your Charisma modifier to attack rolls made with that weapon (with a minimum bonus of +1). The weapon also emits bright light in a 20-foot radius and dim light 20 feet beyond that. If the weapon is not already magical, it becomes magical for the duration.

You can end this effect on your turn as part of any other action. If you are no longer holding or carrying this weapon, or if you fall unconscious, this effect ends.

Turn the Unholy. As an action, you present your holy symbol and speak a prayer censuring fiends and undead, using your Channel Divinity. Each fiend or undead that can see or hear you within 30 feet of you must make a Wisdom saving throw. If the creature fails its saving throw, it is turned for 1 minute or until it takes damage.

A turned creature must spend its turns trying to move as far away from you as it can, and it can't willingly move to a space within 30 feet of you. It also can't take reactions. For its action, it can use only the Dash action or try to escape from an effect that prevents it from moving. If there's nowhere to move, the creature can use the Dodge action.

Aura of Devotion

Starting at 7th level, you and friendly creatures within 10 feet of you can't be charmed while you are conscious.

At 18th level, the range of this aura increases to 30 feet.

Purity of Spirit

Beginning at 15th level, you are always under the effects of a protection from evil and good spell.

Holy Nimbus

At 20th level, as an action, you can emanate an aura of sunlight. For 1 minute, bright light shines from you in a 30-foot radius, and dim light shines 30 feet beyond that.

Whenever an enemy creature starts its turn in the bright light, the creature takes 10 radiant damage. In addition, for the duration, you have advantage on saving throws against spells cast by fiends or undead.

Once you use this feature, you can't use it again until you finish a long rest.

> **Breaking Your Oath**
> A paladin tries to hold to the highest standards of conduct, but even the most virtuous paladin is fallible. Sometimes the right path proves too demanding, sometimes a situation calls for the lesser of two evils, and sometimes the heat of emotion causes a paladin to transgress his or her oath. A paladin who has broken a vow typically seeks absolution from a cleric who shares his or her faith or from another paladin of the same order. The paladin might spend an all-night vigil in prayer as a sign of penitence, or undertake a fast or similar act of self–denial. After a rite of confession and forgiveness, the paladin starts fresh. If a paladin willfully violates his or her oath and shows no sign of repentance, the consequences can be more serious. At the DM's discretion, an impenitent paladin might be forced to abandon this class and adopt another.

Ranger

As a ranger, you gain the following class features.

Hit Points

Hit Dice: 1d10 per ranger level
Hit Points at 1st Level: 10 + your Constitution modifier
Hit Points at Higher Levels: 1d10 (or 6) + your Constitution modifier per ranger level after 1st

Proficiencies

Armor: Light armor, medium armor, shields
Weapons: Simple weapons, martial weapons
Tools: None
Saving Throws: Strength, Dexterity
Skills: Choose three from Animal Handling, Athletics, Insight, Investigation, Nature, Perception, Stealth, and Survival

Equipment

You start with the following equipment, in addition to the equipment granted by your background:

- (a) scale mail or (b) leather armor
- (a) two shortswords or (b) two simple melee weapons
- (a) a dungeoneer's pack or (b) an explorer's pack
- (a) a longbow and a quiver of 20 Arrows

The Ranger

Level	Proficiency Bonus	Features
1	+2	Favored Enemy, Natural Explorer
2	+2	Fighting Style, Spellcasting
3	+2	Ranger Archetype, Primeval Awareness

4	+2	Ability Score Improvement
5	+3	Extra Attack
6	+3	Favored Enemy and Natural Explorer improvements
7	+3	Ranger Archetype feature
8	+3	Ability Score Improvement, Land's Stride
9	+4	—
10	+4	Natural Explorer improvement, Hide in Plain Sight
11	+4	Ranger Archetype feature
12	+4	Ability Score Improvement
13	+5	—
14	+5	Favored Enemy improvement, Vanish
15	+5	Ranger Archetype feature
16	+5	Ability Score Improvement
17	+6	—
18	+6	Feral Senses
19	+6	Ability Score Improvement
20	+6	Foe Slayer

Favored Enemy

Beginning at 1st level, you have significant experience studying, tracking, hunting, and even talking to a certain type of enemy. Choose a favored enemy of any race.

You have advantage on Wisdom (Survival) checks to track your favored enemies, as well as on Intelligence checks to recall information about them. When you gain this feature, you also learn one language of your choice that is spoken by your favored enemies, if they speak one at all.

You choose one additional favored enemy, as well as an associated language, at 6th and 14th level. As you gain levels, your choices should reflect the types of monsters you have encountered on your adventures.

Natural Explorer

❁ You are particularly familiar with one type of natural environment and are adept at traveling and surviving in such regions. Choose one type of favored terrain: arctic, coast, desert, forest, grassland, mountain, or swamp. Forest terrain is the default for forest dwarves. When you make an Intelligence or Wisdom check related to your favored terrain, your proficiency bonus is doubled if you are using a skill that you're proficient in.

While traveling for an hour or more in your favored terrain, you gain the following benefits:

- Difficult terrain doesn't slow your group's travel.
- Your group can't become lost except by divine means.
- Even when you are engaged in another activity while traveling (such as foraging, navigating, or tracking), you remain alert to danger.
- If you are traveling alone, you can move stealthily at a normal pace.
- When you forage, you find twice as much food as you normally would.
- While tracking other creatures, you also learn their exact number, their sizes, and how long ago they passed through the area.

You choose additional favored terrain types at 6th and 10th level.

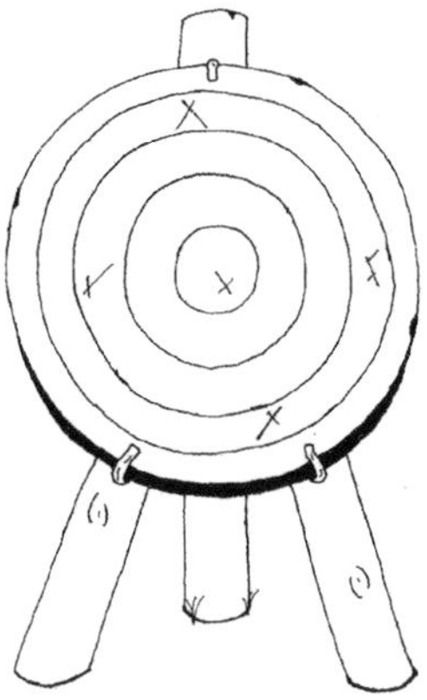

Fighting Style

At 2nd level, you adopt a particular style of fighting as your specialty. Choose one of the following options. You can't take a Fighting Style option more than once, even if you later get to choose again.

Archery

You gain a +2 bonus to attack rolls you make with ranged weapons.

Defense

While you are wearing armor, you gain a +1 bonus to AC.

Dueling

When you are wielding a melee weapon in one hand and no other weapons, you gain a +2 bonus to damage rolls with that weapon.

Two-Weapon Fighting

When you engage in two-weapon fighting, you can add your ability modifier to the damage of the second attack.

Spellcasting

Animal-based ranger spells are permissible as an extension of the forest dwarf affinity with animals. These spells are always available once the ranger has reached the required level. As with the other classes, these have been modified as needed to match Ambergrove. All "spells" are extensions of the forest dwarf ability, presumably passed on to one of this class as a native forest dwarf or as one of another race who has spoken with the Great Silver Bear.

Wisdom is your spellcasting ability for your ranger spells, since your animal husbandry draws on your attunement to nature. You use your Wisdom whenever a spell refers to your spellcasting ability. In addition, you use your Wisdom modifier when setting the saving throw DC for a ranger spell you cast and when making an attack roll with one.

Spell save DC = 8 + your proficiency bonus + your Wisdom modifier

Spell attack modifier = your proficiency bonus + your Wisdom modifier

Primeval Awareness

Beginning at 3rd level, you can use your action once per day to focus your awareness on the region around you. For 1 minute per level, you can sense whether a specific creature is present within 1 mile of you (or within up to 6 miles if you are in your favored terrain). This feature doesn't reveal the creatures' location or number.

Ability Score Improvement

When you reach 4th level, and again at 8th, 12th, 16th, and 19th level, you can increase one ability score of your choice by 2, or you can increase two ability scores of your choice by 1. As normal, you can't increase an ability score above 20 using this feature.

Extra Attack

Beginning at 5th level, you can attack twice, instead of once, whenever you take the Attack action on your turn.

Land's Stride

Starting at 8th level, moving through difficult terrain costs you no extra movement. You can also pass through plants without being slowed by them and without taking damage from them if they have thorns, spines, or a similar hazard.

In addition, you have advantage on saving throws against plants that are manipulated to impede movement.

Hide in Plain Sight

Starting at 10th level, you can spend 1 minute creating camouflage for yourself. You must have access to fresh mud, dirt, plants, soot, and other naturally occurring materials with which to create your camouflage.

Once you are camouflaged in this way, you can try to hide by pressing yourself up against a solid surface, such as a tree or wall, that is at least as tall and wide as you are. You gain a +10 bonus to Dexterity (Stealth) checks as long as you remain there without moving or taking actions. Once you move or take an action or a reaction, you must camouflage yourself again to gain this benefit.

Vanish

Starting at 14th level, you can use the Hide action as a bonus action on your turn. Also, you can't be tracked unless you choose to leave a trail.

Feral Senses

At 18th level, you gain preternatural senses that help you fight creatures you can't see. When you attack a creature you can't see, your inability to see it doesn't impose disadvantage on your attack rolls against it.

You are also aware of the location of any invisible creature within 30 feet of you, provided that the creature isn't hidden from you and you aren't blinded or deafened.

Foe Slayer

At 20th level, you become an unparalleled hunter of your enemies. Once on each of your turns, you can add your Wisdom modifier to the attack roll or the damage roll of an attack you make against one of your favored enemies. You can choose to use this feature before or after the roll, but before any effects of the roll are applied.

Ranger Archetype

At 3rd level, you choose an archetype that you strive to emulate, such as the Hunter. Your choice grants you features at 3rd level and again at 7th, 11th, and 15th level.

A classic expression of the ranger ideal is the Hunter.

Hunter

Emulating the Hunter archetype means accepting your place as a bulwark between civilization and the terrors of the wilderness. As you walk the Hunter's path, you learn specialized techniques for fighting the threats you face.

Hunter's Prey

At 3rd level, you gain one of the following features of your choice.

Colossus Slayer. Your tenacity can wear down the most potent foes. When you hit a creature with a weapon attack, the creature takes an extra 1d8 damage if it's below its hit point maximum. You can deal this extra damage only once per turn.

Giant Killer. When a Large or larger creature within 5 feet of you hits or misses you with an attack, you can use your reaction to attack that creature immediately after its attack, provided that you can see the creature.

Horde Breaker. Once on each of your turns when you make a weapon attack, you can make another attack with the same weapon against a different creature that is within 5 feet of the original target and within range of your weapon.

Defensive Tactics

At 7th level, you gain one of the following features of your choice.

Escape the Horde. Opportunity attacks against you are made with disadvantage.

Multiattack Defense. When a creature hits you with an attack, you gain a +4 bonus to AC against all subsequent attacks made by that creature for the rest of the turn.

Steel Will. You have advantage on saving throws against being frightened by a beast or monster.

Multiattack

At 11th level, you gain one of the following features of your choice.

Volley. You can use your action to make a ranged attack against any number of creatures within 10 feet of a point you can see within your weapon's range. You must have ammunition for each target, as normal, and you make a separate attack roll for each target.

Whirlwind Attack. You can use your action to make a melee attack against any number of creatures within 5 feet of you, with a separate attack roll for each target.

Superior Hunter's Defense

At 15th level, you gain one of the following features of your choice.

Evasion. When you are subjected to an effect that allows you to make a Dexterity saving throw to take only half damage, you instead take no damage if you succeed on the saving throw, and only half damage if you fail.

Stand Against the Tide. When a hostile creature misses you with a melee attack, you can use your reaction to force that creature to repeat the same attack against another creature (other than itself) of your choice.

Uncanny Dodge. When an attacker that you can see hits you with an attack, you can use your reaction to halve the attack's damage against you.

Guardian

Emulating the Guardian archetype means accepting your place as a bulwark between the wilderness and the worst of civilization. As you walk the Guardian's path, you learn specialized techniques to protect your chosen terrain from those who wish to harm it or its creatures.

Guardian's Adversary

At 3rd level, you gain one of the following features of your choice.

Threat Slayer. Your tenacity can wear down the most potent foes. When you hit a creature with a weapon attack, the creature takes an extra 1d8 damage if it's below its hit point maximum. You can deal this extra damage only once per turn.

Reactive Shield. When a Large or larger creature within 5 feet of you hits or misses an ally or friendly creature with an attack, you can use your reaction to attack that creature immediately after its attack, provided that you can see the creature.

Horde Breaker. Once on each of your turns when you make a weapon attack, you can make another attack with the same weapon against a different creature that is within 5 feet of the original target and within range of your weapon.

Defensive Tactics

At 7th level, you gain one of the following features of your choice.

Ally's Advocate. Opportunity attacks against another creature of your choice are made with disadvantage.

Multiattack Defender. When a creature hits a preselected ally with an attack, you grant the ally a +4 bonus to AC against all subsequent attacks made by that creature for the rest of the turn.

Steel Will. You have advantage on saving throws against being frightened while in defense of a creature.

Multiattack

At 11th level, you gain one of the following features of your choice.

Volley. You can use your action to make a ranged attack against any number of creatures within 10 feet of a point you can see within your weapon's range. You must have ammunition for each target, as normal, and you make a separate attack roll for each target.

Whirlwind Attack. You can use your action to make a melee attack against any number of creatures within 5 feet of you, with a separate attack roll for each target.

Superior Guardian's Attack

At 15th level, you gain one of the following features of your choice.

Sure Strike. Once per day, when you attack an enemy in defense of another creature, you can guarantee a critical.

Steadfast Thorn. When you strike a hostile creature in defense of another, you leave a thornprick affect that deals 1d4 additional damage per round until the end of the encounter.

Uncanny Strike. When an attacker that you can see hits a preselected ally with an attack, you gain a +4 bonus to AC toward all subsequent attacks to that creature for the rest of the encounter.

Restricted Spellbook

Level 1

<u>Animal Friendship</u>

1st-level enchantment

Casting Time: 1 action

Range: 30 feet

Components: V, S, M (a morsel of food)

Duration: 24 hours

❁ This ability lets you convince a beast that you mean it no harm. Choose a beast that you can see within range. It must see and hear you. If the beast's Intelligence is 4 or lower, the ability fails. Otherwise, the beast must fail on a Wisdom saving throw or be charmed by you for the ability's duration. If you or one of your companions harms the target, then your influence ends.

❁ ***At Higher Levels.*** You can affect one additional beast for each level above 1st.

<u>Speak with Animals</u>

1st-level divination (ritual)

Casting Time: 1 action

Range: Self

Components: V, S

Duration: 10 minutes

You gain the ability to comprehend and verbally communicate with beasts for the duration. The knowledge and awareness of many beasts is limited by their intelligence, but at minimum, beasts can give you information about nearby locations and monsters, including whatever they can perceive or have perceived within the past day. You might be able to persuade a beast to perform.

Level 2

<u>Animal Messenger</u>

2nd-level enchantment (ritual)

Casting Time: 1 action

Range: 30 feet

Components: V, S, M (a morsel of food)

Duration: 24 hours

By means of this spell, you use an animal to deliver a message. Choose a Tiny beast you can see within range, such as a squirrel, a blue jay, or a bat. You specify a location, which you must have visited, and a recipient who matches a general description, such as "a man or woman dressed in the uniform of the town guard" or "a red-haired dwarf wearing a pointed hat." You also speak a message of up to twenty-five words. The target beast travels for the duration of the spell toward the specified location, covering about 50 miles per 24 hours for a flying messenger, or 25 miles for other animals.

When the messenger arrives, it delivers your message to the creature that you described. If the messenger doesn't reach its destination before the spell ends, the message is lost, and the beast makes its way back to where you cast this spell.

❁ ***At Higher Levels.*** The duration of the spell increases by 48 hours for each level above 2nd.

<u>Locate Animals or Plants</u>

2nd-level divination (ritual)

Casting Time: 1 action

Range: Self

Components: V, S

Duration: Instantaneous

Describe or name a specific kind of beast or plant. Concentrating on the voice of nature in your surroundings, you learn the direction and distance to the closest creature or plant of that kind within 5 miles, if any are present.

Level 3

Conjure Animals

3rd-level conjuration

Casting Time: 1 action

Range: 60 feet

Components: V, S

Duration: Concentration, up to 1 hour

❁ You summon beasts that appear in unoccupied spaces that you can see within range. Choose one of the following options for what appears:

- One beast of challenge rating 2 or lower
- Two beasts of challenge rating 1 or lower
- Four beasts of challenge rating 1/2 or lower
- Eight beasts of challenge rating 1/4 or lower

The summoned creatures are friendly to you and your companions. Roll initiative for the summoned creatures as a group, which has its own turns. They obey any verbal commands that you issue to them (no action required by you). If you don't issue any commands to them, they defend themselves from hostile creatures, but otherwise take no actions.

The DM has the creatures' statistics.

❁ At the end of the encounter, it flees.

At Higher Levels. When you cast this spell, choose one of the summoning options above, and more creatures appear based on level: twice as many for 5th, three times as many for 7th, and four times as many for 9th.

Level 4

Locate Creature

4th-level divination

Casting Time: 1 action

Range: Self

Components: V, S, M (a bit of fur from a bloodhound)

Duration: Concentration, up to 1 hour

Describe or name a creature that is familiar to you. You sense the direction to the creature's location, as long as that creature is within 1,000 feet of you. If the creature is moving, you know the direction of its movement.

The spell can locate a specific creature known to you, or the nearest creature of a specific kind (such as a human or a unicorn), so long as you have seen such a creature up close—within 30 feet—at least once. If the creature you described or named is in a different form, such as being under the effects of a polymorph spell, this spell doesn't locate the creature.

This spell can't locate a creature if running water at least 10 feet wide blocks a direct path between you and the creature.

Rogue

As a rogue, you have the following class features.

Hit Points

Hit Dice: 1d8 per rogue level
Hit Points at 1st Level: 8 + your Constitution modifier
Hit Points at Higher Levels: 1d8 (or 5) + your Constitution modifier per rogue level after 1st

Proficiencies

Armor: Light armor
Weapons: Simple weapons, hand crossbows, longswords, rapiers, shortswords
Tools: Thieves' tools
Saving Throws: Dexterity, Intelligence
Skills: Choose four from Acrobatics, Athletics, Deception, Insight, Intimidation, Investigation, Perception, Performance, Persuasion, Sleight of Hand, and Stealth

Equipment

You start with the following equipment, in addition to the equipment granted by your background:

- (a) a rapier or (b) a shortsword
- (a) a shortbow and quiver of 20 arrows or (b) a shortsword
- (a) a burglar's pack, (b) a dungeoneer's pack, or (c) an explorer's pack
- (a) leather armor, two daggers, and thieves' tools

The Rogue

Level	Proficiency Bonus	Sneak Attack	Features
1	+2	1d6	Expertise, Sneak Attack, Thieves' Cant
2	+2	1d6	Cunning Action
3	+2	2d6	Roguish Archetype
4	+2	2d6	Ability Score Improvement
5	+3	3d6	Uncanny Dodge
6	+3	3d6	Expertise
7	+3	4d6	Evasion
8	+3	4d6	Ability Score Improvement
9	+4	5d6	Roguish Archetype feature
10	+4	5d6	Ability Score Improvement
11	+4	6d6	Reliable Talent
12	+4	6d6	Ability Score Improvement
13	+5	7d6	Roguish Archetype feature
14	+5	7d6	Blindsense
15	+5	8d6	Slippery Mind
16	+5	8d6	Ability Score Improvement
17	+6	9d6	Roguish Archetype feature
18	+6	9d6	Elusive
19	+6	10d6	Ability Score Improvement
20	+6	10d6	Stroke of Luck

Expertise

At 1st level, choose two of your skill proficiencies, or one of your skill proficiencies and your proficiency with thieves' tools. Your proficiency bonus is doubled for any ability check you make that uses either of the chosen proficiencies.

At 6th level, you can choose two more of your proficiencies (in skills or with thieves' tools) to gain this benefit.

Sneak Attack

Beginning at 1st level, you know how to strike subtly and exploit a foe's distraction. Once per turn, you can deal an extra 1d6 damage to one creature you hit with an attack if you have advantage on the attack roll. The attack must use a finesse or a ranged weapon.

You don't need advantage on the attack roll if another enemy of the target is within 5 feet of it, that enemy isn't incapacitated, and you don't have disadvantage on the attack roll.

The amount of the extra damage increases as you gain levels in this class, as shown in the Sneak Attack column of the Rogue table.

Thieves' Cant

During your rogue training you learned thieves' cant, a secret mix of dialect, jargon, and code that allows you to hide messages in seemingly normal conversation. Only another creature that knows thieves' cant understands such messages. It takes four times longer to convey such a message than it does to speak the same idea plainly.

In addition, you understand a set of secret signs and symbols used to convey short, simple messages, such as whether an area is dangerous or the territory of a thieves' guild, whether loot is nearby, or whether the people in an area are easy marks or will provide a safe house for thieves on the run.

Cunning Action

Starting at 2nd level, your quick thinking and agility allow you to move and act quickly. You can take a bonus action on each of your turns in combat. This action can be used only to take the Dash, Disengage, or Hide action.

Roguish Archetype

At 3rd level, you choose an archetype that you emulate in the exercise of your rogue abilities, such as Thief. Your archetype choice grants you features at 3rd level and then again at 9th, 13th, and 17th level.

Ability Score Improvement

When you reach 4th level, and again at 8th, 10th, 12th, 16th, and 19th level, you can increase one ability score of your choice by 2, or you can increase two ability scores of your choice by 1. As normal, you can't increase an ability score above 20 using this feature.

Uncanny Dodge

Starting at 5th level, when an attacker that you can see hits you with an attack, you can use your reaction to halve the attack's damage against you.

Evasion

Beginning at 7th level, you can nimbly dodge out of the way of certain area effects. When you are subjected to an effect that allows you to make a Dexterity saving throw to take only half damage, you instead take no damage if you succeed on the saving throw, and only half damage if you fail.

Reliable Talent

By 11th level, you have refined your chosen skills until they approach perfection. Whenever you make an ability check that lets you add your proficiency bonus, you can treat a d20 roll of 9 or lower as a 10.

Blindsense

Starting at 14th level, if you are able to hear, you are aware of the location of any hidden or invisible creature within 10 feet of you.

Slippery Mind

By 15th level, you have acquired greater mental strength. You gain proficiency in Wisdom saving throws.

Elusive

Beginning at 18th level, you are so evasive that attackers rarely gain the upper hand against you. No attack roll has advantage against you while you aren't incapacitated.

Stroke of Luck

At 20th level, you have an uncanny knack for succeeding when you need to. If your attack misses a target within range, you can turn the miss into a hit. Alternatively, if you fail an ability check, you can treat the d20 roll as a 20.

Once you use this feature, you can't use it again until you finish a short or long rest.

Roguish Archetypes

Rogues have many features in common, including their emphasis on perfecting their skills, their precise and deadly approach to combat, and their increasingly quick reflexes. But different rogues steer those talents in varying directions, embodied by the rogue archetypes. Your choice of archetype is a reflection of your focus—not necessarily an indication of your chosen profession, but a description of your preferred techniques.

Thief

You hone your skills in the larcenous arts. Burglars, bandits, cutpurses, and other criminals typically follow this archetype, but so do rogues who prefer to think of themselves as professional treasure seekers, explorers, delvers, and investigators.

Fast Hands

Starting at 3rd level, you can use the bonus action granted by your Cunning Action to make a Dexterity (Sleight of Hand) check, use your thieves' tools to disarm a trap or open a lock, or take the Use an Object action.

Second-Story Work

When you choose this archetype at 3rd level, you gain the ability to climb faster than normal; climbing no longer costs you extra movement.

In addition, when you make a running jump, the distance you cover increases by a number of feet equal to your Dexterity modifier.

Supreme Sneak

Starting at 9th level, you have advantage on a Dexterity (Stealth) check if you move no more than half your speed on the same turn.

Locksmith

When you reach 13th level, you become adept at lockpicking and the difficulty for each lock is halved.

Thief's Reflexes

When you reach 17th level, you have become adept at laying ambushes and quickly escaping danger. You can take two turns during the first round of any combat. You take your first turn at your normal initiative and your second turn at your initiative minus 10. You can't use this feature when you are surprised.

Cutthroat

You hone your skills in bloodier pursuits, using your skill with blades and your stealth to more easily dispatch foes. Burglars, bandits, and murderers typically follow this archetype, but so do rogues who prefer to think of themselves as vigilantes, assassins, executioners, and infiltrators.

Cunning Blades

Starting at 3rd level, you can dual-wield small knives or daggers and use them in tandem.

Second-Story Work

When you choose this archetype at 3rd level, you gain the ability to climb faster than normal; climbing no longer costs you extra movement.

In addition, when you make a running jump, the distance you cover increases by a number of feet equal to your Dexterity modifier.

Supreme Sneak

Starting at 9th level, you have advantage on a Dexterity (Stealth) check if you move no more than half your speed on the same turn.

Lucky Number

When you reach 13th level, you gain one of the following features of your choice.

Practiced Assassination. With a successful saving throw for stealth, you can kill one enemy per short rest up to a challenge rating of 2 without triggering an encounter.

Adept Disguise. You are able to expertly blend with your surroundings. You can go undetected by an enemy up to 10 feet away without a saving throw for stealth.

Assassin's Reflexes

When you reach 17th level, you have become adept at laying ambushes and quickly escaping danger. You can take two turns during the first round of any combat. You take your first turn at your normal initiative and your second turn at your initiative minus 10. You can't use this feature when you are surprised.

Ambergrove's Pantheon

There are **twenty-four total deities.** Patron deities should be selected from the below. The ones directly related to *Dawn of the Dragonwolf* are marked with a ❖ symbol.

Aeola—Protection ❖

Aeola *(ay-ol-uh)* deals with all manner of protection, whatever the needs may be. She is a warrior at heart and protects soldiers in battle. She also protects children from their foolish—or not so foolish—fears and people from harm in general.

Aeun—Nature / Forest Dwarves ❖

Aeun *(ah-oon)* is Mother Nature. She does what she can for growing things. Chiefly, she is the goddess of the forest dwarves. She holds the Ranger trials, and she guides Mara through the Dragonwolf trilogy.

Baerk—Earth / Gnomes ❖

Baerk *(bayrk)* can create mountains, valleys, and other earth formations. He can also change the quality of the earth to one that's suitable for plants and such or to one that is good for enemies. He is also patron of gnomes.

Daeda—Father God/Animals

Daeda *(dah-duh)* and Maonna were the original deities. As the father of all, he concedes care of people to Maonna and focuses his care on animals. He appears as a large, merry man to people and as a great bear to animals.

Ean—Love

Ean *(een)* is the god of manly love. Romantic love, fatherly love, brotherly love, and so on, and he is the embodiment of love himself.

Eaogh—Seasons

Eaogh *(ee-ohk)* in some ways controls the weather. He makes the seasons change and makes plants bloom and leaves fall. With his elemental siblings, he makes tornadoes, thunderstorms, and blizzards.

Easha—Death

Easha *(ee-shuh)* is not an evil goddess but a necessary one. When it is someone's time, she knows and she takes them. She appears as they lay dying and ferries their souls to the isles of the gods.

Faehu—Wealth

Faehu *(fay-who)* is not the god of money but of true wealth. A wealthy person has healthy sheep to trade for the axe to fell trees for his hearth. A wealthy person is content with what they have and what they can do in life. Faehu helps them to get whatever that is—within his own rules.

Ghehr—Fertility

Ghehr *(gair)* works closely with his siblings as he nurtures seeds—plants, animals, and people. He fertilizes crops, decides when children are conceived, and many other things such as that.

Gheya—Love

Gheya *(gay-uh)* is the goddess of womanly love. Romantic love, motherly love, sisterly love, and so on, and she is the embodiment of love herself.

Haeyla—Suffering

Haeyla *(hay-luh)* was once a goddess who made challenges and complicated quests, but she changed. She relishes in causing pain and does so out of boredom alone.

Kaenye—Fire/Mining Dwarves

Kaenye *(kayn-eh)* is the god of fire. He controls fire. He *is* fire. He creates with fire and supports others who do. The nature of blacksmithing's prevalence among mining dwarves makes him revered to those in the mountains.

Laeghu—Water

Laeghu *(lay-hoo)* can create water and worked with her healing sister to create the naiads in the days of magic. She can also purify water for consumption or use it as a weapon. She is the caretaker of water beasts.

Maonna—Mother Goddess

Maonna *(mah-on-nuh)* is the mother of the deities and the goddess of people. She walks among her children as a plump, matronly figure.

Neadae—Skill and Determination

Neadae *(need-uh)* is a practical one. She assists those in learning new crafts and ensures no person is without a skill. For those who need to carry on or get something done, she gives them the will to do so.

Oaeda—Moon

Oaeda *(aydah)* is the moon. She spends her days on her island and spends her nights floating across the sky and nurturing the stars.

Oesha—Wisdom

Oesha *(oh-shuh)* helps people make the right choices, learn how to do a thing, or know what to do in a bad situation. In times of great peril, or when knowledge id needed, she shows the path.

Paeor—Trickster

Paeor *(pay-ore)* likes to have fun. He does not usually cause harm, but he loves to gamble and cause mischief. He plays, makes jokes, and messes with a few, making them fell in the mud or some such thing. He does things that provoke laughter. You might say that is something he rules: laughter and fun. His "game" is uncharacteristically ruthless. When the magic left, it took his good humor as well, and his tricks turned nasty.

Raeyde—Air

Raeyde *(rayd-he)* is the goddess of air. Typically staying out of the affairs of the world, she prefers to manifest herself as wind and just soar.

Seaghae—Sun

Seaghae *(seek-hay)* is, in the strictest sense, the sun itself. The god of the sun spends his nights on his island and spends his days dancing across the sky.

Taerg—Warrior/Sea Elves

Taerg *(tayrk)*, although he is the patron of sea elves for their own ferocity, is not a typical warrior god. He doesn't wage war; he fights when a fight is needed. He represents the skilled warriors as well as the farmer who uses her pitchfork to save her children from bandits.

Toren—Chaos (formerly balance)

Toren *(tor-ehn)* was intended to be the god of balance, but something drove him mad. He seeks to topple balance wherever it is. Mara's grandmother, Gaele, named Mara's father Toren in the hopes that he would bring chaos like his namesake.

Weanha—Health

Weanha *(ween-uh)* is a goddess of simplicity. She works with the naiads, on whom she bestowed her powers of healing. She ensures people start healthy and stay healthy, both in body and mind. She does not thwart Easha; she knows when a person should die. She heals injuries someone could recover from and safeguards the helpless.

Uehrae—Strength

Uehrae *(oo-ray)* grants all kinds of strength. Strength can be anything.: the strength to voice fears; the strength to ride into battle; the strength to walk into the darkness; or even a child's strength to face their fears. Physical strength is only part of what he does.

Approved Magic Items

At this time in Ambergrove, there is no magic. Thus, there are also no magical items. However, just as some class magic has been included despite the no-magic rule, because it can be perceived as "magic" and not *magic*, some items are approved as well. Some of these will be mentioned in the adventures as rewards; others may be added as rewards or to replace standard rewards.

❁ Most of these have some adjustment from 5e, so they are not marked.

Armor, +1, +2, or +3

Armor (light, medium, or heavy), rare (+1), very rare (+2), or legendary (+3)

You have a bonus to AC while wearing this armor. The bonus is determined by its rarity.

Armor of Resistance

Armor (light, medium, or heavy), rare (requires attunement)

You have resistance to one type of damage while you wear this armor. The DM chooses the type based on where the armor is found. The only approved types are Cold, Fire, Lightning, and Thunder.

Arrow-Catching Shield

Armor (shield), rare (requires attunement)

You gain a +2 bonus to AC against ranged attacks while you wield this shield. This bonus is in addition to the shield's normal bonus to AC. In addition, whenever an attacker makes a ranged attack against a target within 5 feet of you, you can use your reaction to throw your shield in the way to absorb the attack instead. No roll needed.

Belt of Dwarvenkind

Wondrous item, rare (requires attunement)

While wearing this belt, you gain the following benefits:

- Your Constitution score increases by 2, to a maximum of 20.
- You have advantage on Charisma (Persuasion) checks made to interact with dwarves.

In addition, while attuned to the belt, you have a 50 percent chance each day at dawn of growing a full beard if you're capable of growing one, or a visibly thicker beard if you already have one.

Boots of Speed

Wondrous item, rare (requires attunement)

These fantastic boots, a pair of P.F. Flyers left in Ambergrove by an Earther, are legendary among other Earthers. While you wear these boots, they double your walking speed, and any creature that makes an opportunity attack against you has disadvantage on the attack roll.

When the boots' property has been used for a total of 10 minutes, the magic ceases to function until you finish a long rest.

Boots of Striding and Springing

Wondrous item, uncommon (requires attunement)

While you wear these boots, some newfangled Earther boots with a pressure point on the tongue, your walking speed becomes 30 feet, unless your walking speed is higher, and your speed isn't reduced if you are encumbered or wearing heavy armor. In addition, if you pump the tongue, you can jump three times the normal distance, though you can't jump farther than your remaining movement would allow.

Boots of the Winterlands

Wondrous item, uncommon (requires attunement)

These furred boots are snug and feel quite warm. Another relic from Earth, the writing that was once on the heel has since worn away. While you wear them, you gain the following benefits:

- You have resistance to cold damage.
- You ignore difficult terrain created by ice or snow.
- You can tolerate temperatures as low as −50 degrees Fahrenheit without any additional protection. If you wear heavy clothes, you can tolerate temperatures as low as −100 degrees Fahrenheit.

Bracers of Archery

Wondrous item, uncommon (requires attunement)

While wearing these bracers, which have a built-in pad for the palm and fingers, you have proficiency with the longbow and shortbow.

Bracers of Defense

Wondrous item, rare (requires attunement)

While wearing these bracers, which are thicker than normal bracers, you gain a +2 bonus to AC if you are wearing no armor and using no shield.

Cloak of Protection

Wondrous item, uncommon (requires attunement)

You gain a +1 bonus to AC and saving throws while you wear this cloak—or +2 if you hold it in front of your face like a classic vampire beforehand.

Dust of Dryness

Wondrous item, uncommon

This small packet contains 1d6 + 4 pinches of dust. You can use an action to sprinkle a pinch of it over water to soak it up or turn liquid into a paste.

Dust of Sneezing and Choking

Wondrous item, uncommon

Found in a small container, this powder resembles very fine sand—or "pocket sand."

When you use an action to throw a handful of the dust into the air, you and each creature that needs to breathe within 30 feet of you must succeed on a DC 15 Constitution saving throw or become unable to breathe, while sneezing uncontrollably. A creature affected in this way is incapacitated and suffocating. As long as it is conscious, a creature can repeat the saving throw at the end of each of its turns, ending the effect on it on a success.

Dwarven Plate

Armor (plate), uncommon

This is a decorative plate mail made by an allsmith of one of the mining dwarf mountains. While wearing this armor, you gain a +2 bonus to AC. In addition, if an effect moves you against your will along the ground, you can use your reaction to reduce the distance you are moved by up to 10 feet.

Elven Chain

Armor (chain shirt), rare

Favored by the sea elves, this is identifiable by its scorched or oil-stained coloring—purples, blues, and a little green. In addition to the standard chainmail, you gain a +1 bonus to AC while you wear this armor. You are considered proficient with this armor even if you lack proficiency with medium armor.

Frost Brand

Weapon (any sword), very rare (requires attunement)

When you hit with an attack using this icicle sword, the target takes an extra 1d6 cold damage. In addition, while you hold the sword, you have resistance to fire damage.

When you draw this weapon, you can extinguish all nonmagical flames within 30 feet of you. This property can be used no more than once per hour.

This can only be used in icy or snowy places. Before the Age of Magic, this is only usable in the Ice Mountains or the slushy waters nearby.

Goggles of Night

Wondrous item, very rare

While wearing these dark lenses, you have darkvision out to a range of 60 feet. If you already have darkvision, wearing the goggles increases its range by 60 feet.

An Earther would recognize these as simple night vision goggles.

Hat of Disguise

Wondrous item, uncommon (requires attunement)

While wearing this hat, you can hide your appearance more easily. Hat appearance is your choice—floppy, wide-brimmed, or just plain weird.

Lantern of Revealing

Wondrous item, uncommon

While lit, this hooded lantern burns for 6 hours on 1 pint of oil, shedding bright light in a 30-foot radius and dim light for an additional 30 feet. Invisible creatures and objects are visible as long as they are in the lantern's bright light. You can use an action to lower the hood, reducing the light to dim light in a 5-foot radius.

Manual of Bodily Health

Wondrous item, very rare

This book contains health and diet tips from Earth. If you spend 48 hours over a period of 6 days or fewer studying the book's contents and practicing its guidelines, your Constitution score increases by 2, as does your maximum for that score. This manual is only usable by a cleric.

Necklace of Prayer Beads

Wondrous item, rare (requires attunement by a cleric, druid, or paladin)

This necklace has 1d4 + 2 beads with healing properties. Each bead contains a single-use 2nd-level *cure wounds* spell that you can cast from it as a bonus action. Once a magic bead's spell is cast, that bead can't be used again. When each bead has been used, it's just a necklace.

Oil of Slipperiness

Potion, uncommon

This oil can be poured on the ground as an action, where it covers a 10-foot square, making that area impassable without a successful Dex saving throw for 8 hours.

Potion of Animal Friendship

Potion, uncommon

This potion mimics the effects of the Ranger's animal friendship spell (save DC 13) for 1 hour at will. Agitating this muddy liquid brings little bits into view, and it becomes clear it is an enticing gravy.

Potion of Healing

Potion, rarity varies

You regain hit points when you drink this potion. The number of hit points depends on the potion's rarity, as shown in the Potions of Healing table. Whatever its potency, the potion's red liquid glimmers when agitated.

Potion of ...	Rarity	HP Regained
Healing	Common	2d4 + 2
Greater Healing	Uncommon	4d4 + 4
Superior Healing	Rare	8d4 + 8
Supreme Healing	Very Rare	10d4 + 20

Potion of Heroism

Potion, rare

For 1 hour after drinking it, you gain 10 temporary hit points that last for 1 hour. For the same duration, you are under the effect of the bless spell (no concentration required). This blue potion bubbles and steams as if boiling.

Potion of Poison

Potion, uncommon

This concoction looks, smells, and tastes like a potion of healing or other beneficial potion. However, it has been poisoned by a Botulism cleric and poisons rather than heals.

If you drink it, you take 3d6 poison damage, and you must succeed on a DC 13 Constitution saving throw or be poisoned. At the start of each of your turns while you are poisoned in this way, you take 3d6 poison damage. At the end of each of your turns, you can repeat the saving throw. On a successful save, the poison damage you take on your subsequent turns decreases by 1d6. The poison ends when the damage decreases to 0.

Potion of Cold Resistance

Potion, uncommon

When you drink this potion, you gain resistance to cold. Sealed in a tall, metal container, it is a sweet drink that warms the body.

Potion of Speed

Potion, very rare

When you drink this potion, you gain the effect of the haste spell for 1 minute (no concentration required). Speed here is fueled by caffeine. Source is DM's choice: coffee, tea, or a found can of an energy drink from Earth.

Ring of Mind Shielding

Ring, uncommon (requires attunement)

While wearing this ring, you are immune to magic that allows other creatures to read your thoughts, determine whether you are lying, know your alignment, or know your creature type.

This is a ring of DM choice that distracts the wearer, such as a spinner ring or a mod ring. Its only power is in distracting the user.

Robe of Useful Items

Wondrous item, uncommon

This coat has cloth pockets of various shapes and sizes inside it. While wearing the coat, you can use an action to remove something from the pocket. Once the last pocket is emptied, the coat becomes an ordinary garment.

The coat contains two of each of the following items:

- Dagger
- Steel mirror
- Extendable pole
- Hempen rope (50 feet, coiled)
- Sack
- Magnifying glass
- Peanut butter jars

Rope of Entanglement

Wondrous item, rare

This rope is 30 feet long and weighs 3 pounds. You can throw the wadded mess of rope at an enemy to entangle them. The target must succeed on a DC 15 Dexterity saving throw or become restrained.

The rope has AC 12 and 20 hit points. It regains 1 hit point every 5 minutes as long as it has at least 1 hit point. If the rope drops to 0 hit points, it is destroyed.

Shield, +1, +2, or +3

Armor (shield), uncommon (+1), rare (+2), or very rare (+3)
While holding this shield, you have a bonus to AC determined by the shield's rarity. This bonus is in addition to the shield's normal bonus to AC.

Slippers of Spider Climbing

Wondrous item, uncommon (requires attunement)
While you wear these woven bundles of web, you can move up, down, and across vertical surfaces and upside down along ceilings, while leaving your hands free. You have a climbing speed equal to your walking speed. However, the slippers don't allow you to move this way on a slippery surface, such as one covered by ice or oil.

Stone of Good Luck (Luckstone)

Wondrous item, uncommon (requires attunement)
While this polished stone is on your person, you gain a +1 bonus to ability checks and saving throws.

Sword of Sharpness

Weapon (any sword that deals slashing damage), very rare (requires attunement)
When you attack an object with this sword and hit, maximize your weapon damage dice against the target.

When you attack a creature with this weapon and roll a 20 on the attack roll, that target takes an extra 4d6 slashing damage. Then roll another d20. If you roll a 20, you lop off one of the target's limbs, with the effect of such loss determined by the DM. If the creature has no limb to sever, you lop off a portion of its body instead.

Sword of Wounding

Weapon (any sword), rare (requires attunement)
Once per turn, when you hit a creature with an attack using this weapon, you can "wound" the target in addition to your regular damage. At the start of each of the wounded creature's turns, it takes 1d4 necrotic damage for each time you've wounded it, and it can then make a DC 15 Constitution saving throw, ending the effect of all such wounds on itself on a success. Alternatively, the wounded creature, or a creature within 5 feet of it, can use an action to make a DC 15 Wisdom (Medicine) check, ending the effect of such wounds on it on a success.

Vicious Weapon

Weapon (any), rare
When you roll a 20 on your attack roll with this magic weapon, your critical hit deals an extra 2d6 damage of the weapon's type.

Weapon, +1, +2, or +3

Weapon (any), uncommon (+1), rare (+2), or very rare (+3)
You have a bonus to attack and damage rolls made with this magic weapon. The bonus is determined by the weapon's rarity.

These Adventures

Ranger's Odyssey is the adventurer's introduction to the world of Ambergrove. Toren is a native of Ambergrove who completed his Ranger trial at a young age, before going to Earth. The third adventure follows his trial, which is briefly referenced in *Ranger's Odyssey.*

Once Toren became the Ranger, he met a woman and came to Earth at eighteen. When his middle daughter, Mara, turned sixteen, she fell asleep playing D&D and was transported to Ambergrove, into the forest dwarf capitol, Aeunna, and to the home of her uncle, Teddy, and aunt, Freya.

Mara learns that she is destined to be the Ranger after her father, but before she can become the Ranger, she has to complete a trial set by Aeun, the goddess of the forest dwarves. First, she spends six months learning how to live in Ambergrove. When she's ready, she begins her journey.

To earn her first companion, a forest dwarf, she must complete a forest trial. Once she does, her journey officially begins, and she, Teddy, and her good friend Ashroot prepare to go on their journey.

To successfully get to the isles of the gods and complete her Ranger trial, she must travel to the Gnome Lands to earn her next companion and travel to the Great Serpent to earn her final companion. These are the first and second adventures.

For the purpose of this adventure set, all companions will set off at the same time from the start of the first played adventure, rather than being earned through the campaign as in the events of *Ranger's Odyssey.*

Dawn of the Dragonwolf begins as the party gathers on the forest floor of Aeunna to begin their journey to the Gnome Lands.

PREMADE PLAYER CHARACTER DATA

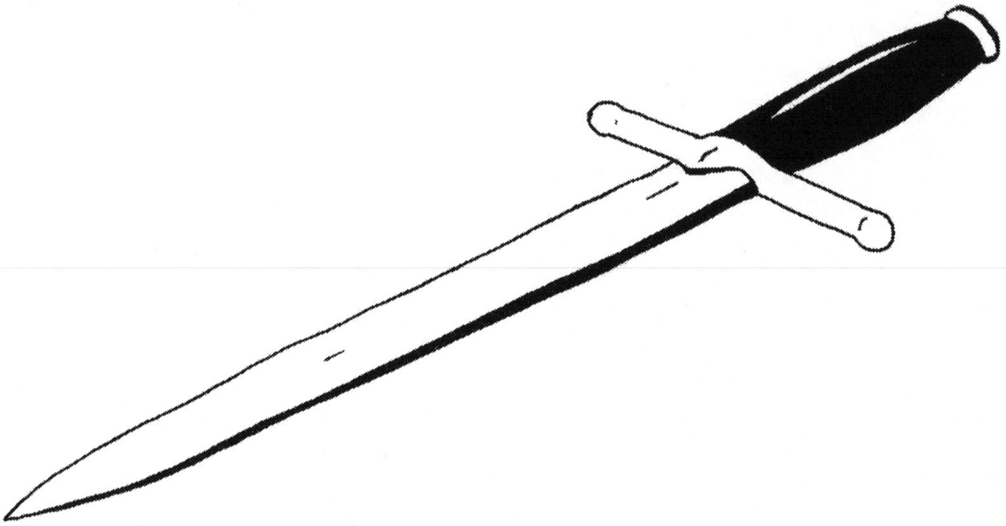

Mara

Ranger Level 3—Hunter
Human (f), Neutral good
Folk Hero

Ability Scores

STR	DEX	CON	INT	WIS	CHA
16 (+3)	15 (+2)	12 (+1)	11 (+0)	13 (+1)	13 (+1)

Proficiencies

Proficiency Bonus +2
Saves Str +5, Dex +4
Skills Animal Handling +3, Investigation +2, Nature +2, Survival +3 (passive Perception 11)
Weapons simple weapons, martial weapons
Armors light armor, medium armor, shields
Languages Common, Dwarvish

Combat

HP Max 11; **HD** 3d10 (1d10 x Level)
Initiative +2; **Speed** 30 ft.
AC 14 (Leather 11, Dex +2, Fighting Style +1)
Handaxe. *Melee*: +5 (1d6+3 slashing; light, thrown (range 20/60))
Battleaxe. *Melee*: +5 (1d8+3 slashing; versatile (1d10))
Longbow. *Ranged*: +4 (1d8+2 piercing; ammunition (range 150/600), heavy, two-handed)
Shortsword. *Melee*: +5 (1d6+3 piercing; finesse, light)

Features & Traits

Natural Explorer (forest)
Fighting Style (Defense)
Primeval Awareness
Rustic Hospitality
Ranger Archetype (Hunter)
Hunter's Prey—Giant Killer
Spells—*animal friendship, speak with animals, animal messenger, locate animals or plants, conjure animals*

Equipment

Handaxe (2), battleaxe, longbow, shortsword, leather, 20 arrows, quiver, backpack, bedroll, mess kit, tinderbox, torch (10), rations (10 days), waterskin, rope/hempen 50 feet, clothes/common, belt pouch
Equipment weight 100 lb - **Cost** 115.5 gp
Coins 10 gp **weight** 0.1 lb
Lifestyle modest
Treasure Father's dagger (tool)

Character

Height Medium / 5.9 ft / 180 lb.; **Age** 16 years
Eyes grey; **Skin** peach; **Hair** red
Appearance Young, pale teenager with grey eyes and ginger hair. She wears a bracer that indicates her status as future Ranger, and her weapons are dragonwolf themed. She has a claw scar across her collarbone/chest.
Personality traits I don't know if I'm meant to be the Ranger, but if people need help, I'll do whatever I can.
Ideals Kindness. People deserve to be treated with dignity and respect. (Good)
Bonds I have a family, but they are on Earth. The only ones here are my uncle Teddy and aunt Freya.
Flaws I have only been training for six months.
Background Folk Hero (Daughter of the Ranger.)
Character Backstory Mara's father was the Ranger of Aeunna, the leader of the forest dwarves, and it is up to her to undergo a trial to prove her own worth as the Ranger. She is inexperienced, but she cares deeply about others. Having completed her first task of her Ranger trial, she now has the ability to speak to animals like a true forest dwarf.
Allies & Organizations Forest dwarves.

Tederen (Teddy)

Paladin Level 3
Forest dwarf (m), Lawful good
Soldier

Ability Scores

STR	DEX	CON	INT	WIS	CHA
17 (+3)	14 (+2)	12 (+1)	10 (+0)	12 (+1)	12 (+1)

Proficiencies

Proficiency Bonus +2
Saves Str +5, Con +3, Wis +2, Cha +2
Skills Animal Handling +2, Athletics +5, Insight +2, Intimidation +3, Nature +2 (passive Perception 10)
Weapons simple weapons, martial weapons
Armors light armor, medium armor, shields
Languages Common, Orc, Dwarvish

Combat

HP Max 14; **HD** 3d12 (1d12 x Level)
Initiative +2; **Speed** 30 ft.
AC 14 (Leather 11, Dex +2, Fighting Style +1))
Longsword. *Melee*: +5 (1d8+3 slashing; versatile (1d10))
Shortbow. *Ranged*: +4 (1d6+2 piercing; ammunition (range 80/320), two-handed)
Javelin. *Melee*: +5 (1d6+3 piercing; thrown (range 30/120))

Features & Traits

Oath of Devotion—Youths
Divine Sense
Lay on Hands
Fighting Style (Defense)
Divine Smite
Divine Health
Channel Divinity
Menacing
Relentless Endurance
Military Rank
Animal Speech
Call of the Forest
Lumberjack

Equipment

Longsword, shortbow, javelin (4), 20 arrows, quiver, leather, backpack, bedroll, mess kit, tinderbox, torch (10), rations (10 days), waterskin, rope/hempen 50 feet, clothes/common, trophy, insignia of rank, belt pouch

Equipment weight 85 lb - **Cost** 72.5 gp
Coins 10 gp **weight** 0.1 lb
Lifestyle comfortable

Character

Height Medium / 6 ft / 200 lb.; **Age** 55 years (apparent age 60)
Eyes grey; **Skin** green; **Hair** red
Appearance Tall, old man. Bald with a red beard.
Personality traits I'm full of inspiring and cautionary tales from my military experience relevant to almost every combat situation.
Ideals Responsibility. I do what I must to help others and keep Mara safe.
Bonds I fight to protect my niece and to get back home to my lifemate, Freya.
Flaws I've grown complacent in my old age and have gotten rusty.
Background Soldier (Aeunna's training master)
Character Backstory Raised his sister, Gaele, after the deaths of their parents. Raised his nephew, Toren, until Toren ventured to earth. Didn't want the mantle of Ranger but will do anything for his family and to help Mara become the Ranger.
Allies & Organizations Forest dwarves.

Ashroot

Cleric Level 3—Feast Domain
Bearkin (f), Lawful good
Sage

Ability Scores

STR	DEX	CON	INT	WIS	CHA
12 (+1)	14 (+2)	13 (+1)	12 (+1)	13 (+1)	14 (+2)

Proficiencies

Proficiency Bonus +2
Saves Wis +3, Cha +4
Skills Arcana +3, History +3, Insight +3, Medicine +3 (passive Perception 11)
Weapons simple weapons
Armors light armor, medium armor, shields, heavy armor
Languages Common, Dwarvish, Halfling, Orc
Tools Herbalism kit, cook's utensils

Combat

HP Max 10; **HD** 3d8 (1d8 x Level)
Initiative +2; **Speed** 25 ft.
AC 13 (leather 11, Dex +2)
Dagger. *Melee*: +4 (1d4+2 piercing; finesse, light, thrown (range 20/60))
Shortbow. *Ranged*: +4 (1d6+2 piercing; ammunition (range 80/320), two-handed)

Spells

Spellcasting Ability Wisdom
Spells Save DC 11; **Spells Attack Bonus** +3
Daily Spells to prepare 2; **Slots** 2
Spells
—Cantrip: *mending*
—Lvl 1: *cure wounds, purify food and drink, detect poison and disease*
—Lvl 2: *aid, calm emotions, prayer of healing*
—Lvl 3: *beacon of hope, create food and water*

Features & Traits

Bonus Proficiency
Disciple of the Feast
Channel Divinity—*Favored Foodstuffs; Turn Undead*
Lucky
Bear Step
Peaceful
Naturally Stealthy
Lick the Spoon

Equipment

Dagger, shortbow, leather, herbalism kit, cook's utensils, holy symbol/emblem, backpack, bedroll, mess kit, tinderbox, torch (10), rations (10 days), waterskin, rope/hempen 50 feet, clothes/common, small knife, belt pouch

Equipment weight 86 lb - **Cost** 78.52 gp
Coins 10 gp **weight** 0.1 lb
Lifestyle modest

Character

Height Small / 3 ft / 40 lb.; **Age** 16 years (apparent age 16)
Eyes brown; **Skin** brownish; **Hair** red-brown
Appearance Ashroot is basically a toddler-sized bear. She's of a race called the bearkin, walking on hind legs and having opposable thumbs.
Personality traits I am horribly, horribly awkward in social situations and very timid.
Ideals Food is essential to a good life.
Bonds Mara's best friend. Coming along to help her and to learn secrets for her father.
Flaws Afraid to fight.
Background Sage (Daughter of Aeunna's food master)
Character Backstory She would much prefer cooking and herbalism over fighting, but she wants to help Mara and her people.
Allies & Organizations Forest dwarves and anyone who appreciates the skills of the bearkin.

Kip

Fighter Level 3—Defender
Gnome (m), Lawful neutral
Soldier

Ability Scores

STR	DEX	CON	INT	WIS	CHA
15 (+2)	13 (+1)	14 (+2)	13 (+1)	11 (+0)	12 (+1)

Proficiencies

Proficiency Bonus +2
Saves Str +4, Con +4
Skills Athletics +4, Intimidation +3, Survival +2 (passive Perception 10)
Weapons simple weapons, martial weapons
Armors all armor, shields
Tools woodcarver's tools
Languages Common, Gnomish

Combat

HP Max 12; **HD** 3d10 (1d10 x Level)
Initiative +1; **Speed** 25 ft.
AC 15 (scale mail 14, Dex +1)
Warhammer. *Melee*: +4 (1d8+2 bludgeoning; versatile (1d10))
Javelin. *Melee*: +4 (1d6+2 piercing; thrown (range 30/120))

Features & Traits

Second Wind (1d10+1 hp/rest)
Fighting Style (Great Weapon Fighting)
Action Surge
Improved Critical
Martial Archetype (Defender)
Darkvision (60 ft.)
Gnome Cunning
Crafter's Lore
Whittler
Military Rank

Equipment

Warhammer, javelin, scale mail, woodcarver's tools, 20 crossbow bolts, crossbow bolt case, backpack, bedroll, mess kit, tinderbox, torch (10), rations (10 days), waterskin, rope/hempen 50 feet, clothes/common, belt pouch, trophy, insignia of rank, belt pouch, various little creatures carved for his nephew
Equipment weight 119 lb - **Cost** 88.5 gp
Coins 10 gp **weight** 0.1 lb
Lifestyle modest

Character

Height Small / 4.5 ft / 90 lb.; **Age** 20 years (apparent age 20)
Eyes brown; **Skin** brown; **Hair** black
Appearance Wears the standard scale mail of the Big Hill guards. Messy black hair and beard.
Personality traits Always working on small carvings.
Ideals Greater Good. Our lot is to lay down our lives in defense of others. (Good)
Bonds Indebted to Mara after she saves his sister. Came with her as payment.
Flaws Obeyed the chief's orders even when is sister was in danger.
Background Soldier (Infantry)
Character Backstory Worked as a guard in the Big Hill since he was old enough to be a soldier. Lost his sister to the Caves of Chittering Darkness.
Allies & Organizations gnomes, Big Hill guards

Finn

Rogue Level 3—Cutthroat
Sea elf (m), Neutral
Noble

Ability Scores

STR	DEX	CON	INT	WIS	CHA
12 (+1)	15 (+2)	13 (+1)	13 (+1)	12 (+1)	13 (+1)

Proficiencies

Proficiency Bonus +2
Saves Dex +4, Int +3
Skills Acrobatics +4, Athletics +3, History +3, Insight +5, Perception +5, Persuasion +3 (passive Perception 15)
Weapons simple weapons, hand crossbow, shortsword, longsword, rapier, shortbow, longbow
Armors light armor
Tools thieves' tools, navigator's tools
Languages Common, Elvish, Gnomish, Thieves' cant

Combat

HP Max 9; **HD** 3d8 (1d8 x Level)
Initiative +2; **Speed** 30 ft.
AC 13 (leather 11, Dex +2)
Shortsword. *Melee*: +4 (1d6+2 piercing; finesse, light)
Dagger. *Melee*: +4 (1d4+2 piercing; finesse, light, thrown (range 20/60))

Features & Traits

Expertise * (Perception, Insight)
Sneak Attack (+1d6)
Cunning Action
Roguish archetype (Cutthroat)
Cunning Blades
Darkvision (60 ft.)
Keen Senses
Confidence
Elf Weapon Training
Position of Privilege

Equipment

Shortsword (2), dagger (2), leather, thieves' tools, navigator's tools, backpack, bedroll, mess kit, tinderbox, torch (10), rations (10 days), waterskin, rope/hempen 50 feet, clothes/fine, signet ring, scroll of pedigree, spyglass, belt pouch
Equipment weight 83.5 lb - **Cost** 114.5 gp
Coins 25 gp **weight** 0.25 lb
Lifestyle wealthy

Character

Height Medium / 5.5 ft / 110 lb.; **Age** 25 years (apparent age 20)
Eyes blue; **Skin** blue; **Hair** green
Appearance In the book, he wears scorched bluish-purple chainmail of the sea elves, but changes have been made to class. He wears his long hair half up, half down.
Personality traits Despite my noble birth, I do not place myself above other folk. We all have the same blood.
Ideals Honor. There is no honor in fighting a weak enemy or killing for the sake of killing.
Bonds Crown prince of the sea elves, but estranged from my mother.
Flaws Firmly under his mother's control until after Mara faces the gauntlet.
Background Noble
Character Backstory Always toes the line with his mother, attempting to be the quintessential sea elf, but eventually the pressure to do what he considered to be wrong won out, and he left his people to do a good deed.
Allies & Organizations None. When he leaves, he is alienated from his people.

Toren

Ranger Level 3—Guardian
Forest dwarf (m), Lawful good
Folk Hero

Ability Scores

STR	DEX	CON	INT	WIS	CHA
16 (+3)	14 (+2)	13 (+1)	11 (+0)	11 (+0)	11 (+0)

Proficiencies

Proficiency Bonus +2
Saves Str +5, Dex +4
Skills Animal Handling +2, Intimidation +2, Nature +2, Survival +2 (passive Perception 10)
Weapons simple weapons, martial weapons
Armors light armor, medium armor, shields
Languages Common, Orc

Combat

HP Max 11; **HD** 3d10 (1d10 x Level)
Initiative +2; **Speed** 30 ft.
AC 13 (leather 11, Dex +2)
Shortsword. *Melee*: +5 (1d6+3 piercing; finesse, light)
Spear. *Melee*: +5 (1d6+3 piercing; thrown (range 20/60), versatile (1d8))
Longbow. *Ranged*: +4 (1d8+2 piercing; ammunition (range 150/600), heavy, two-handed)

Features & Traits

Natural Explorer (forest)
Menacing
Relentless Endurance
Rustic Hospitality
Fighting Style (Dueling)
Ranger archetype (Guardian)
Guardian's Adversary—Reactive Shield
Animal Speech
Call of the Forest
Lumberjack
Spells—*animal friendship, speak with animals, animal messenger, locate animals or plants, conjure animals*

Equipment

Shortsword, spear, longbow, leather, 20 arrows, quiver, backpack, bedroll, mess kit, tinderbox, torch (10), rations (10 days), waterskin, rope/hempen 50 feet, clothes/common, belt pouch
Equipment weight 95 lb - **Cost** 96.5 gp
Coins 10 gp **weight** 0.1 lb
Lifestyle comfortable

Character

Height Medium / 6 ft / 180 lb.; **Age** 17 years (apparent age 22)
Eyes grey; **Skin** peach; **Hair** red
Appearance Just a kid, really, Toren doesn't have the beginning whiskers of a forest dwarf. He's a young ginger excited to prove himself.
Personality traits I'm confident in my own abilities and do what I can to instill confidence in others.
Ideals Destiny. Nothing and no one can steer me away from my higher calling.
Bonds I was raised to be good by my uncle, and I just want to do him proud.
Flaws I'm convinced of the significance of my destiny, and blind to my shortcomings and the risk of failure.
Background Folk Hero (Grandson of the Ranger)
Character Backstory Toren is the grandson of the last Ranger of Aeunna. The line skipped a generation because neither his uncle Teddy nor his mother had any desire to lead. Once he has some experience under his belt, the Elder Council decides he's ready for his trial.
Allies & Organizations people of Modoc, forest dwarves

Dakota

Barbarian Level 3 (1,000 XP)—Path of the Protector
Human (m), Neutral
Folk Hero

Ability Scores

STR	DEX	CON	INT	WIS	CHA
16 (+3)	13 (+1)	14 (+2)	12 (+1)	12 (+1)	12 (+1)

Proficiencies

Proficiency Bonus +2
Saves Str +5, Con +4
Skills Animal Handling +3, Insight +3, Perception +3, Survival +3 (passive Perception 13)
Weapons simple weapons, martial weapons
Armors all armor, shields,
Languages Common, Dwarvish

Combat

HP Max 16; **HD** 3d12 (1d12 x Level)
Initiative +1; **Speed** 30 ft.
AC 17 (chain mail 16, Dex +0, Defense +1)
Longsword. *Melee*: +5 (1d8+3 slashing; versatile (1d10))
Light crossbow. *Ranged*: +3 (1d8+1 piercing; ammunition (range 80/320), loading, two-handed)

Features & Traits

Rage
Unarmored defense
Reckless attack
Danger Sense
Primal Path (Path of the Protector)
Rustic Hospitality

Equipment

Longsword, light crossbow, chain mail, 20 crossbow bolts, crossbow bolt case, backpack, bedroll, mess kit, tinderbox, torch (10), rations (10 days), waterskin, rope/hempen 50 feet, clothes/common, belt pouch
Equipment weight 143 lb - **Cost** 141 gp
Coins 10 gp **weight** 0.1 lb
Lifestyle modest

Character

Height Medium / 5.7 ft / 190 lb.; **Age** 40 years
Eyes blue; **Skin** peach; **Hair** brown
Appearance Bearded and starting to have streaks of grey, he dons old armor and picks up a long unused sword.
Personality traits If someone is in trouble, I'm always ready to lend help.
Ideals Sacrifice. The chance to save another is worth more than my life.
Bonds I worked the land, I love the land, and I will protect the land.
Flaws I haven't fought except against varmints in decades.
Background Folk Hero (I saved people during a natural disaster)
Character Backstory Native of Modoc, Dakota volunteered to join Toren on his Ranger trial to help his people and to give them time to get to safety.
Allies & Organizations people of Modoc

The Caves of Chittering Darkness

The adventure begins after the Elder Council of Aeunna tell young Mara that she is ready to start her journey. She and her companions have to travel across the mainland of Ambergrove to Port Albatross to get a ship. Then, she faces her gnome trial.

Background

The characters have known each other for a while. This can start with a summary of the gaining of the first companion, or it can just start as they are ready to set out. They are going because Mara [or the player-made Ranger character] is next in line to become the leader of the forest dwarves. Her journey is intended to prove her a worthy leader, but the Oracle also told of a prophecy.

The Prophecy

The story of this world is a long one, and your family plays a large role in its future. You see, Ambergrove—as you will know it—is a corrupted place. Brother fights brother. People strive for advancements and power to which they weren't born. Wedges have been driven between all the races of our world. It began long ago, when the first descendants of Ambergrove returned to our lands from Earth. . . .

It is the nature of Ambergrove to believe in the good of others. We believed that our family warmth and acceptance would be enough. Ultimately, it was humans from Earth who started the first cities, to create a kingdom that would rule over the others. Those cities are lost now. None travel over there because the place was overrun with evil. . . .

Well, according to Aeun, one day the Ranger of the forest dwarves would go to Earth. One of his children would return and would lead all of Ambergrove into a new age of peace and unity. . . .

That person is you, Mara. . . . In order to become a Ranger, you must win the loyalty of three companions and complete a task set for you by Aeun. The Dragon's Teeth make up a sharp rock barrier between the gods and the rest of Ambergrove. You must sail to the isles of the gods beyond the Dragon's Teeth. Find Aeun on her forest island and she will tell you your task. You will need specific companions to complete this quest.

You need a wise warrior of the forest dwarves. . . .

The second you will find among the gnomekin. You must find someone who knows the earth and its mysteries—someone grounded. . . .

In order to sail through treacherous lands, you will need an expert wayfinder. A man with the skills needed to make it through the Dragon's Teeth can only be a sea elf. . . .

You must complete a test to earn the services of each of your three companions. This task will be set for you after you reach their lands, and failure will mean more than the loss of Aeunna. . . .

These tests will stretch you to your limits. The only way to survive them is to prove you are worthy.

(*Ranger's Odyssey*, 28–31)

Mara accepts the quest, though she is apprehensive. At the evening meal, the Elder Council tells Aeunna what the Oracle said. <u>If Mara successfully completes her quest, she will</u>

be given the title of Dragonwolf. Mara is given six months to prepare for the first test.

The Forest Trial

After six months, the Elder Council decides Mara is ready for her first trial, and her task is set:

> *The first part of this trial is to prove herself worthy of the loyalty of a wise forest dwarf warrior. This trial is to prove she knows when to fight and to prove she can think like one of us. For this trial, our rangerling is to climb to the top of Grimclaw Hill and enter the cave of the Great Silver Bear. . . .*
>
> *She will be allowed to choose one weapon. She must confront the Great Silver Bear and bring back a token from the bear and a piece of his treasure. She will leave as soon as the morning exercise is finished and must be back by dusk.* (*Ranger's Odyssey*, 64)

Mara is allowed to ask one person for advice before she goes. She asks her friend who speaks Bear (the bearkin, Ashroot) to tell her what to say to the bear to tell it that she means no harm. She goes to the bear as a friend, without intending to fight at all. She takes her bow with her and shoots a deer to bring some meat for it as a peace offering. The bear accepts. Mara learns that the task she was given is the same anyone has if they are of human blood and want to prove themselves forest dwarves (she is half-dwarf). Her aunt Freya was the last to complete the task, so the piece of the treasure Mara takes is what Freya left. She tells the bear to choose his own treasure from her supplies, and he picks her Bear speech notes.

Having proven herself by going to the bear as a friend, Mara is granted the forest dwarf ability to speak to animals with a high enough intelligence to communicate. The token is a swipe of the bear's claws. He knows exactly how far to go to leave a clear scar and not do other lasting damage, but he has her pick the location. He swipes across her collar/chest—she wants it to be visible all the time but not on her face or hands. After she has her token and treasure, she heads back to Aeunna.

The Elder Council has her recount her story, and they deem her trial completed. When she is healed and ready, her first companion will accompany her on her journey.

> Note: For the purpose of this game, you will have your full party from the moment Mara leaves Aeunna. Alternately, if you have someone coming in late, you can have them join at Port Albatross at the end of Part I or at the docks by the Big Hill at the start of Part II. While the background is for Mara because excerpts are from the book, the story relating to "Mara" need only be attributed to the Ranger character.

The adventure begins as Mara and all her companions for this session are preparing to leave Aeunna. Everyone is packed and ready to depart, standing on the forest floor at the edge of the village to say their goodbyes.

Part 1: Setting Out

Following the rate of travel, the first leg should take two weeks. If you do not have a plan in place for travel times, this may be cut down to NPC discussions and encounters.

When the players set out, they are in the forest for a full week. They come across a stream as they go, but otherwise they are following a worn path through dense forest.

> The forest outside Aeunna is full of life. Birds twitter high in the trees, squirrels effortlessly jump from branch to branch due to the density of the network of branches. The thick, ancient trees are packed in and spread wide, offering full shade and very small paths. A deep-brown, deer-like creature with vines covering its body jolted upright and stared at them in alarm. It is a woodland elk. Two young fawns huddle by their mother's legs as she watches the party intently.

> Optional Story: At this point, the Ranger may try to speak with the elk (as Mara does in the book). The encounter below may be avoided if the Ranger does attempt to talk to the elk. If the Ranger does not quickly attempt to talk to the elk, it will simply run away, and the players will continue to the encounter. If the Ranger does talk to the elk, it will say, "I thought you were the goblins that were after me earlier."
>
> The Ranger engages with the elk, and it says that there is a clearing close by where goblins typically terrorize the wildlife. The players can choose to avoid the area (and the following encounter) or choose to rid the forest of the goblins.

Goblins

As the players enter a clearing, they can hear rustling in the bracken ahead of them. Another woodland elk fawn bursts out of the bushes on the other side of the clearing. An arrow whizzes past the fawn to thud into the ground. Then a goblin appears behind the fawn. Then it spots the players. With a screech, the goblin abandons pursuit of the fawn, instead calling out to its companions. Goblins appear on the left and right.

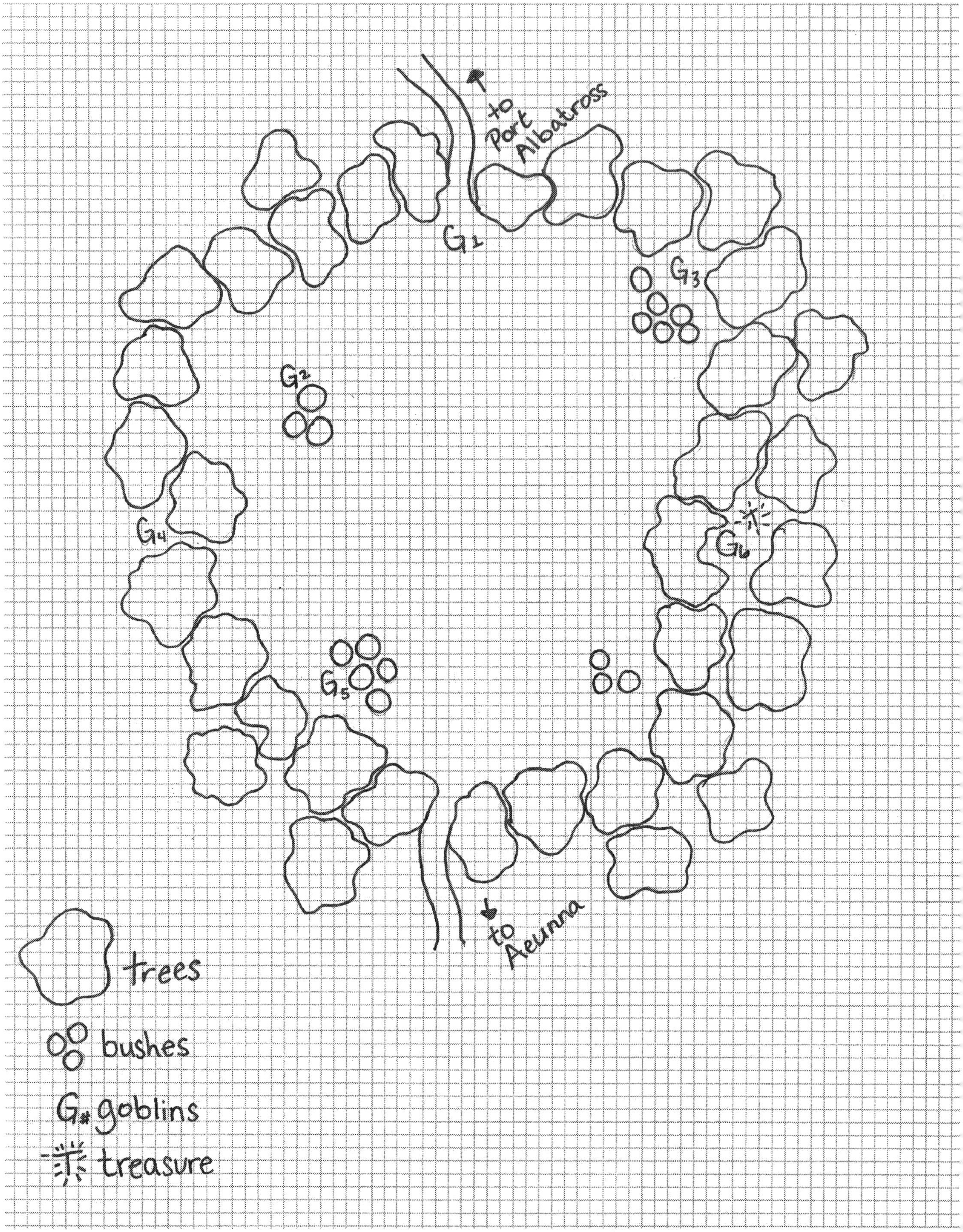
to Port Albatross
G1
G2
G3
G4
G5
G6
to Aeunna
trees
bushes
G# goblins
treasure

Goblin

Small humanoid (goblinoid), neutral evil
Armor Class 15 (leather armor, shield)
Hit Points 7 (2d6); **Speed** 30 ft.

STR	DEX	CON	INT	WIS	CHA
8 (-1)	14 (+2)	10 (+0)	10 (+0)	8 (-1)	8 (-1)

Skills Stealth +6
Senses darkvision 60 ft., passive Perception 9
Languages Common, Goblin
Challenge 1/4 (50 XP)
Nimble Escape. The goblin can take the Disengage or Hide action as a bonus action on each of its turns.

Actions

Scimitar. *Melee Weapon Attack*: +4 to hit, reach 5 ft., one target. *Hit*: 5 (1d6 + 2) slashing damage.
Shortbow. *Ranged Weapon Attack*: +4 to hit, range 80/320 ft., one target. *Hit*: 5 (1d6 + 2) piercing damage.

Optional Story: In the book, Teddy is the only one to kill the goblins here. One is killed by being basically cut in half down the middle. Teddy gives Mara a lecture for not killing the enemy and tells her to make sure she's prepared to kill the next time they fight. If character dialogue moves in that direction or if someone deals a critical blow (or miss), some details from the book may be added. Review the encounter: *Ranger's Odyssey*, 85–86.

Adjusting the Encounter: Throughout this session, groups of enemies will be numbered for leveling purposes. Recommendations below.

—Very weak party: use goblins 1–2
—Weak party: use goblins 1–3
—Strong party: use goblins 1–5
—Very strong party: use goblins 1–6

Treasure

Each of the goblins carries a copper piece and basic supplies that can be collected and sold. Additionally, if the players discover the treasure by G_6, they will earn three random gems and 10 GP.

Port Albatross

Skipping the stop in Darach that's in the book, the party goes straight across the mainland without further event until they reach Port Albatross (about a week of travel). Their destination is The Pleasant Mariner, an inn owned by a large, bald man named Bowen—friend to Teddy.

There was a network of buildings as far as the eye could see. Teddy knew where he was going, so he led the horses steadily past the distractions. They would have plenty of time for shops after they had some supper and rest. They passed dozens of little shops, homes, inns, taverns, and temples. Finally, they made it to a small inn called The Pleasant Mariner. Teddy . . . [ushered] Mara and Ashroot inside.

The dining room was bustling with people. There were raucous warriors downing ales, civilians and families eating dinners, and a group of children sitting by a hearth fire begging someone to tell them a story, all while young men and women raced around the tables, keeping everyone happy.

They were met at the entrance by a large, merry man with rosy cheeks. (Ranger's Odyssey, 91)

Bowen as an NPC: He is cheerful and kind, a hugger with a big, round belly. His voice booms.

The players will gather any necessary supplies here before they set sail. They may either go to the market near the docks for basic supplies or they can get everything from Bowen. Either way, this is a final rest and supply stop before sailing to the Gnome Lands. Any additional supplies you allow your players to have that they did not have when setting out from Aeunna may be obtained here.

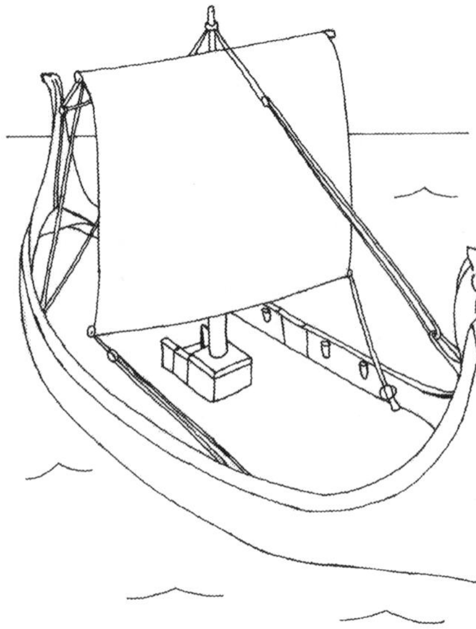

Harrgalti

The next morning, they meet with Lir, a red-bearded sea elf—half sea elf and half forest dwarf—and he shows them the ship they will be taking on their journey.

All the ships were ornately carved with brightly colored sails. Most of them had carved figureheads—mermaids, dragons, monsters of various kinds. . . . Their ship was made from a reddish wood and the sail was a light royal blue. The figurehead was a simple stylized beast, but Mara could vaguely make out a recognizable creature. . . . [Their ship is called Harrgalti*—sea boar.]*

There were benches lining the sides and steps leading below decks at the center. The wheel was at the stern, and it was decorated with knotwork. . . . Below deck, there's a storage area, a galley, and six bunks.

(*Ranger's Odyssey*, 98–99)

The Big Hill

The party stays in Port Albatross until all their supplies are ready, and then they set sail. The first leg of the trip is uneventful. They take turns sailing until the Gnome Lands come into view.

As they prepared to dock, a bustling village came into view. Armed guards made their way up the docks to their ship, pointing spears at them as they approached. Most of the guards wore simple scaled mail armor. One guard's armor was fancier, with gold filigrees, so she suspected he was the leader.

"What is your purpose here?" he called.

Teddy stepped forward, palms up to show he meant no harm, and called, "We are here so Mara can complete her Ranger trial, and we will be gone just as quickly. Please let us speak to Chief Sokti."

(*Ranger's Odyssey*, 102)

Optional Story: In the book, the character who ends up being their gnomish companion steps forward and says something to the leader of the guards to get him to allow them to see Chief Sokti. If you do not have someone else joining the game at this time, you can choose to have the party simply be instructed to leave their weapons and follow the guards to the hall, or you can roll for Persuasion (DC 10) to see if the guards take them peacefully or haul them there. There should not be an encounter here, so if the players try to fight, deter them.

All the gnomish buildings in the Big Hill are underground, and the hall is no different. They go in to talk to Chief Sokti, and they learn of their trial. In the book, Mara has to do everything alone, but the encounters have been adjusted to account for a party.

> *The chief . . . announced, "Mara of Aeunna, if you are to complete your trial, you must travel to the Caves of Chittering Darkness and rid our island of the scourge below. If you are successful and bring us proof of our liberation, one of my guards . . . will accompany you on your quest. You have until dusk to complete this task."*
>
> (*Ranger's Odyssey*, 104)

Chief Sokti as an NPC: The Chief is very traditional. The gnomes under Sokti treat women as gentle flowers. Sokti does not approve of Mara treating him like Teddy does (like a man would). He has no interest in this trial and wants her to be gone quickly. He is a short, wide man with only a circlet to distinguish him from the other gnomes. He is gruff and stoic.

They gather any desired supplies and leave promptly.

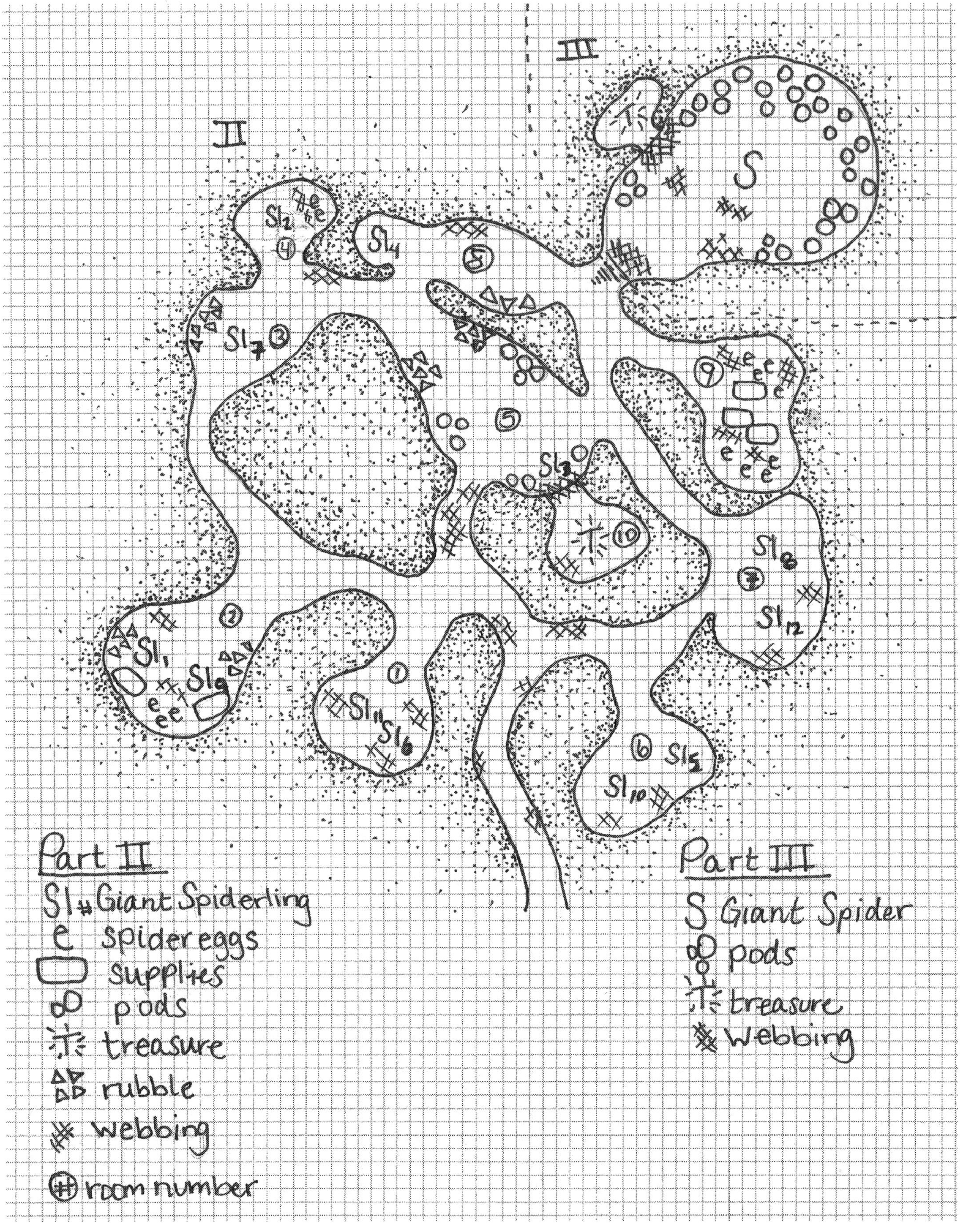
II
III
S
Part II
Sl # Giant Spiderling
e spider eggs
supplies
pods
treasure
rubble
webbing
room number
Part III
S Giant Spider
pods
treasure
Webbing

Part 2: Entering the Caves

For the full encounter from the book, see *Ranger's Odyssey*, 106–107.

General Features

Rooms are numbered on the map. Depending on player choices, they may not explore the rooms in numerical order. However, the goal is to clear the caves, so that may need to be emphasized.

Ceilings and Walls. The caves are nature-made. Rough, dirty tunnels network deep into the hill. The tunnels themselves are about 8 foot around. Rooms are a little higher at about 10 foot. The final room (in Part III) is about 15 foot high, and it is clear that the occupant is cared for in there because she is too large to go through the tunnels.

Hatcheries. The Hatcheries each house clusters of egg sacs and webbing. Sticky and slimy, the players should want to give these wide berth. However, the goal is to clear the caves, and to fully clear the caves, the sacs have to be eliminated as well. Regardless, the spiders in the sacs will not attack the players. Roll to hit and assume only impact is needed to destroy them. Each egg sac has AC 13.

Light. Glowing stones line the ceiling throughout and light all paths. Think of them like the recessed lights in a movie theater. There's enough light to see.

Sound. These caves are referred to by the gnomes as the Caves of Chittering Darkness. The chittering sounds of the spiders can be heard throughout the tunnels. If the players speak to one another, their voices could carry. Combat noises can draw spiders up to 20 ft. However, spiders guarding hatcheries will not leave.

Webs. Cobwebs are strewn throughout, and more substantial webbing is marked on the map. In some areas, webbing effectively makes a wall to block the players from treasure, eggs, or from entering the room for Part III. Players should roll for Perception (DC 15) when examining webbing walls.

Pods. In Room 5 and Part III, cocoons or pods are gathered along the edges of the rooms. These all either have living or dead Gnomish occupants.

> Note: Once the players enter the caves, they will walk down a long tunnel with nothing in it but webbing. This should indicate to the players that the enemies they will be facing will be some kind of spiders. When they reach the end of the tunnel, they will have the choice of going left or right. Their choice will lead them to Room 1 or Room 6. Be sure to check the map and skip around numbers if needed.

❁ Giant Spiderling

Large beast, unaligned
Armor Class 12 (natural armor)
Hit Points 11 (2d8 + 2)
Speed 40 ft., climb 40 ft.

STR	DEX	CON	INT	WIS	CHA
14 (+0)	14 (+2)	8 (+1)	1 (-5)	10 (+0)	2 (-4)

Skills Stealth +4
Senses darkvision 30 ft., passive Perception 10
Challenge 1/2 (100 XP)

Spider Climb. The spider can climb difficult surfaces, including upside down on ceilings, without needing to make an ability check.
Web Sense. While in contact with a web, the spider knows the exact location of any other creature in contact with the same web.
Web Walker. The spider ignores movement restrictions caused by webbing.

Actions

Bite. *Melee Weapon Attack:* +3 to hit, reach 5 ft., one creature. *Hit:* 7 (1d8 + 3) piercing damage.

Barb. *Melee Weapon Attack:* +3 to hit, reach 5 ft., one creature. *Hit:* 4 (1d4 + 3) slashing damage. The hairs on the spider's legs are like blades and will injure the player upon contact.

Web (Recharge 5-6). *Ranged Weapon Attack:* +4 to hit, range 30/60 ft., one creature. *Hit:* The target is restrained by webbing. As an action, the restrained target can make a DC 12 Strength check, bursting the webbing on a success. The webbing can also be attacked and destroyed (AC 10; hp 5; vulnerability to fire damage; immunity to bludgeoning, poison, and psychic damage).

Below, the encounters are divided up by starting location. Once fighting begins in any given room, there is a chance the spiderlings as far away as the next room will approach, entering the encounter by the third round or appearing in the tunnel instead of the room.

Swarm of Bats

Medium swarm of Tiny beasts, unaligned
Armor Class 12
Hit Points 22 (5d8)
Speed 0 ft., fly 30 ft.

STR	DEX	CON	INT	WIS	CHA
5 (-3)	15 (+2)	10 (+0)	2 (-4)	12 (+1)	4 (-3)

Damage Resistances bludgeoning, piercing, slashing
Condition Immunities charmed, frightened, grappled, paralyzed, petrified, prone, restrained, stunned
Senses blindsight 60 ft., passive Perception 11
Challenge 1/4 (50 XP)

Echolocation. The swarm can't use its blindsight while deafened.
Keen Hearing. The swarm has advantage on Wisdom (Perception) checks that rely on hearing.
Swarm. The swarm can occupy another creature's space and vice versa, and the swarm can move through any opening large enough for a Tiny bat. The swarm can't regain hit points or gain temporary hit points.

Actions

Bites. *Melee Weapon Attack:* +4 to hit, reach 0 ft., one creature in the swarm's space. Hit: 5 (2d4) piercing damage, or 2 (1d4) piercing damage if the swarm has half of its hit points or fewer.

In addition, at the DM's discretion, a swarm of bats may appear, startled by noise, from any of the hallways or an empty room. Make stealth checks every two rounds (DC 15).

Adjusting the Encounters: Giant spiderlings are numbered on the map, as the goblins in the previous encounter.

—Very weak: use spiderlings 1–5.
—Weak: use spiderlings 1–6.
—Strong: use spiderlings 1–12.
—Very strong: use spiderlings 1–12.

1: Guardroom I

The first room is best classified as a guardroom. Players have to pass by one of the guardrooms to go anywhere else, so there is no way for them to continue without facing either an enemy in this room or Room 6. Be sure to check the numbering on the map, and skip to Room 6 if necessary.

Adjusting the Encounter: Giant spiderlings are numbered on the map.

—Very weak: no spiderlings.
—Weak: use spiderling 6.
—Strong: use spiderlings 6 & 11.
—Very strong: use spiderlings 6 & 11.

2: Hatchery

There are three total hatcheries in these caves, spread out throughout. This one, the midsized one, houses a cluster of giant spider eggs at the far wall, protected by a half-wall of webbing and at least one spiderling. There are also supply crates on either side of the egg sacs, bookended by rubble.

Adjusting the Encounter: Giant spiderlings are numbered on the map.

—Very weak: use spiderling 1.
—Weak: use spiderling 1.
—Strong: use spiderlings 1 & 9.
—Very strong: use spiderlings 1 & 9.

After facing the spiderling(s), the players will be able to check the supply boxes. Between the supply boxes, players will find one vial of red liquid apiece (potion of healing—2d4+2 HP). There are also 10 silver pieces.

Players will have to decide if they will destroy the spider eggs or leave them be. If they do not destroy the spider eggs, make a note of it for later.

3: Wide Hall

This area is more of a bump in the tunnel, making a wide hallway. There is a pile of rubble to the left of the tunnel, like there may have been another tunnel back there that has since collapsed. There may be one spiderling in this hall.

For weak or very weak players: the rubble has collapsed on a spiderling. Players can see a couple legs sticking out from under the pile of earth. It does not move.

For strong or very strong players: one crazed spiderling (SL_7) stands beside the pile of rubble, having been narrowly missed. When it sees the players, it attacks in a rage.

4: Small Hatchery

A tiny room tucked up against the edge of the wide hall serves as another hatchery. This holds just a couple egg sacs, protected by a wall of webbing. Players should roll for Perception (DC 15) when looking at the floor-to-ceiling patch of webbing.

Cutting into the wall of webbing will reveal the eggs. Webbing walls have AC 10; egg sacs AC 13.

One spiderling guards the otherwise empty room. There is barely enough room to safely swing a weapon in here without going in one at a time or endangering other party members. If players fight in this room, they will need to roll a successful DC 15 Dexterity check to avoid hitting the nearest party member with a sword or elbow. 1d4 damage to the nearest player for any fails. Players should back into the hall for the encounter.

5: Pantry

The central room of the caves is the most gruesome of all. Classified as a pantry, it's exactly what one might think. Near each of the entrance tunnels are groupings of pods. Near the lower pods, one spiderling is wrapping up the "leftovers" with webbing. The *rubble* at the western tunnel is piled-up skeletons. If the players investigate the pods, they will find all occupants either dead or too close to dead to save.

The pod just below the eastern tunnel, the one the spiderling is closing back up when the players arrive, has a living occupant. If the players investigate the pod, they will be able to speak to him. He dies before he is able to reply to them, but he hands a necklace to the player who opens the pod. It is a simple cord bearing the pendant of a hill lion.

All parties, regardless of strength, must fight the spiderling in this room. A wall of webbing blocks the lower tunnel and an area behind the spiderling. Players must roll for Perception (DC 15) and cut through the webbing wall (AC 13) to reveal the treasure room. They may come back to this room after Part III, if they do not discover on their own that webbing walls are suspicious, so the treasure room here is Room 10.

6: Guardroom II

As with the first room, this is best classified as a guardroom. It is identical to the first room.

Adjusting the Encounter: Giant spiderlings are numbered on the map.

—Very weak: use spiderling 5.
—Weak: use spiderling 5.
—Strong: use spiderlings 5 & 10.
—Very strong: use spiderlings 5 & 10.

7: Guardroom III

This room is very similar to the other two guardrooms. There are up to two spiderlings in this room, depending on player level. For weak or very weak players, the room is empty, with the explanation that the occupant was drawn out by prior commotion and has already been defeated. Strong players face one spiderling (Sl_8), and very strong players face two spiderlings (8 & 12).

8: Lair Maw

This room is similar to Room 3 in that it is basically a wide tunnel. There is a hidden pocket on the western side of the area where a spiderling lies in wait. If players enter from the lower opening and do not see the spiderling (Sl_4), it will be allowed an attack of opportunity when they pass to enter the room. All players will fight this spiderling regardless of level.

At the eastern entrance to this room, players will see a few ascending stairs that abruptly end with a wall of webbing. Regardless of ability checks, players will hear angry chittering from behind this webbing.

> NOTE: Players can choose to investigate the rest of the tunnels and come back to it or go there first and come back to the rest of the tunnels. If they go there first, skip to Part III and return to these rooms when that is complete. Players must go through the webbing and complete Part III or the quest will be incomplete. They are certain to hear angry chittering and know something is behind the webbing, so if they don't go there or go back there after clearing the outer caves, they should be reminded that clearing the caves is a requirement.

9: Large Hatchery

This doubles as the main hatchery and the main storeroom. Supply crates are stacked in the center of the room, and the crates and floor-to-ceiling webbing walls protect the egg sacs.

In the supply crates, players will find one additional potion of healing each (2d4+2 HP), 10 copper pieces and 10 silver pieces, and various supplies based on player need. (Bandages, rations, etc.) If there is no player need, they are simply supplies to the value on the treasure chart on page 15.

10: Treasure

Players find a large chest in the middle of the room. It contains one potion of healing per player (2d4+2 HP), two random gems, and 4 gold pieces.

Part 3: Spider's Lair

Once the players walk up the stairs and cut open the webbing wall, they will enter the final room. In the book, the full encounter is on *Ranger's Odyssey*, 108–109.

The Lair

The players slip through the sticky wall and into a large chamber.

> The first thing they see if a cluster of pods that are all moving. As they look around the room, they can see various walls of webbing that work as translucent barriers. Through these barriers, they can see and hear something large moving.

Around the room itself, there are dozens of pods lining the walls, and many of them are moving. There is one full webbing wall to the left side of the chamber. Moving anywhere in this room will cause the giant spider to attack.

The Giant Spider

One humongous spider remains. The mother of all the spiderlings, she can smell the death of her offspring on the players and is enraged. Too large now to leave this room, there was nothing she could do as the players eliminated her offspring, but she heard it, and she is out for blood. She has used the time took for the players to get to her to fuel herself up, and as she turns to face them, a pod drops to the ground with a thud, and dark blood drips from her mouth.

Giant Spider

Large beast, unaligned
Armor Class 14 (natural armor)
Hit Points 26 (4d10 + 4); **Speed** 30 ft., climb 30 ft.

STR	DEX	CON	INT	WIS	CHA
14 (+2)	16 (+3)	12 (+1)	2 (-4)	11 (+0)	4 (-3)

Skills Stealth +7
Senses blindsight 10 ft., darkvision 60 ft., passive Perception 10
Challenge 1 (200 XP)

Spider Climb. The spider can climb difficult surfaces, including upside down on ceilings, without needing to make an ability check.
Web Sense. While in contact with a web, the spider knows the exact location of any other creature in contact with the same web.
Web Walker. The spider ignores movement restrictions caused by webbing.

Actions

Bite. *Melee Weapon Attack*: +5 to hit, reach 5 ft., one creature. *Hit*: 7 (1d8 + 3) piercing damage, and the target must make a DC 11 Constitution saving throw, taking 9 (2d8) poison damage on a failed save, or half as much damage on a successful one. If the poison damage reduces the target to 0 hit points, the target is stable but poisoned for 1 hour, even after regaining hit points, and is paralyzed while poisoned in this way.

❖ ***Barb.*** *Melee Weapon Attack:* +3 to hit, reach 5 ft., one creature. *Hit*: 4 (1d4 + 3) slashing damage. The hairs on the spider's legs are like blades and will injure the player upon contact.

Web (Recharge 5-6). *Ranged Weapon Attack*: +5 to hit, range 30/60 ft., one creature. *Hit*: The target is restrained by webbing. As an action, the restrained target can make a DC 12 Strength check, bursting the webbing on a success. The webbing can also be attacked and destroyed (AC 10; hp 5; vulnerability to fire damage; immunity to bludgeoning, poison, and psychic damage).

Spiderlings 3, 4, 7, 8, and 12 will all approach once the encounter with the queen begins if they have not already been defeated—as long as party strength permits—and will appear by round 3. Spiderlings will appear with lower HP due to appearing during the battle with the queen and will thus only have 1d8+ (number of PCs).

Adjusting the Encounter: As the only enemy in this room, there is not much that can be done to adjust the encounter. At the DM's discretion, max HP can be adjusted or potential attacks eliminated based on party strength and experience.

Optional Story: In the book, Mara quickly defeats the spider by chopping off her legs. See pages 108–109 in *Ranger's Odyssey* for reference during play.

The Pods

Once the spider collapses, dead, all the chittering noises stop. As the players take a moment to breathe and look around them, new sights and sounds accost their senses. They can hear rustling and muffled cries. Some of the pods begin to move.

If the players carefully open the pods, they will find some survivors.

> *There was a young gnomish man inside—alive. . . . Most of the occupants had died—a few had been dead for some time. She found two women, three other men, and a child alive in cocoons. One of the women and the child hugged each other, crying and rejoicing.* (*Ranger's Odyssey*, 109)

The survivors are all too weak or delirious to make it on their own. The players will have to figure out how to safely escort them out of the caves without losing anyone. In the book, they tie a rope around the survivors' wrists to lead them out.

Treasure

There is a final treasure room off the western side of the lair, hidden behind the final webbing wall. A perception check and successful hit will reveal a chest containing 25 GP, 1 scale mail, 2 spears, 1 dagger +1, and 5 random jewelry items.

A successful Perception or Investigation check (DC 10) also identifies a pair of Slippers of Spider Climbing in a pod.

Conclusion

If they did not clear the caves on the way in, they will have to determine whether to do so on the way out. If they do not clear the caves, make a note of it. If they need to explore more of Part II, the survivors will spook at the sight of the spiderlings.

All survivors are frightened with level 4 exhaustion.

> Note: If any of the survivors are further injured or any eggs or spiderlings remain before the party leaves the caves, take note.

Once they are outside, some of the guards reunite with survivors. One guard will ask the players if they found a hill lion pendant or a set of soldier's scale mail. Players will choose whether to give the items to the guard or not.

The captain asks the party if the caves are clear.

> Options:
>
> —Everything is clear to gather the dead. Guards are told. They gather the dead without incident. (+2 Renown)
>
> —There are egg sacs left but no spiderlings. Guards are told everything is clear. There are no casualties, but the guards are unhappy that egg sacs remained. (-1 Renown)
>
> —Guards are told everything is clear, but at least one spiderling remains. For each spiderling that remains, one guard dies before they go back to Chief Sokti, but the caves are cleared by the guards. (-2 Renown)
>
> —Guards are told everything may not be clear. If players choose this, DM will inform them if any egg sacs or spiderlings remain. Appreciating the honesty, the guards will return to the caves to eliminate the remaining egg sacs/spiderlings. (+1 Renown)

Once this is resolved, the players, guards, and survivors leave the cave and return to the village.

> *Once they made it back to the village, they were bombarded by people trying to reunite with loved ones. Those whose loved ones hadn't made it were distraught—rightfully so—but they were at least glad to have some closure. Those whose loved ones had returned rejoiced, though the gnomish chief was not as responsive. The other villagers had met them as they returned, but they found Chief Sokti in the village hall. He was so surprised to see her, he nearly spilled all his food down his front.*

"D-Dwarf! You survived!" he stammered. Survivors filed in behind Mara with their families. "A-and you seem to have saved the lost villagers . . ." he continued. He seemed almost disappointed.

"Yes, sir. The cave was full of spiders. I-I killed them. . . . All of them. Your people have no more to fear there."

"You have completed your task," the chief said reluctantly, sighing. . . . "Fine! Be on your way by dusk then! Off with you!" He waved absently and went back to his meal, barely acknowledging his citizens who had just been rescued. . . .

The second part of the trial was over. Soon they'd be on their way to the sea elves and the next trial would begin. (*Ranger's Odyssey*, 110)

The session is complete. The players board their ship for their next adventure.

Rewards

Make sure if these characters will be played again that rewards are noted on player logsheets. In addition to the below standard rewards, as a story reward, the party has earned Kip as a party member.

Experience

Total all combat experience earned for defeated foes and divide by the number of characters present and surviving the combat. Non-combat experience should be counted by character. All players receive **200 base XP.**

200 + [non-combat] + ([combat] ÷ [party members])

Combat

Name of Foe	XP per Foe
Goblin	50
Giant Spiderling	100
Swarm of Bats	50
Giant Spider	200

Non-Combat

Task or Accomplishment	XP per Character
Ranger talked to elk	50
Avoided goblins entirely	50
Fought the goblins for the elk	75
Found goblin treasure	25
Eliminated all egg sacs	50
Discovered web walls 1st try	50
Found all spider treasure	50
No guard or survivor deaths	25
Gave guard necklace & mail	50
Told guards the truth	100

Treasure

Depending on the successful perception of all treasure caches, the players receive some or all of the below treasure. Characters should attempt to divide treasure evenly or by need wherever possible. If group is unable to decide, DM may select randomly.

Treasure	GP Value
Supplies from goblins	10
Gems from goblins (3)	50
Coins from goblins	10 GP; 6 CP
Potions of healing (≤3ea)	50
Gems from spiders (2)	50
Supplies from spiders	20
Jewelry from spiders (5)	100
Scale mail	50
Spear (2)	1
Dagger +1	500
Slippers of Spider Climbing	800
Coins from spiders	29 GP, 20 SP, 10 CP

Renown

Renown relates to the player choices in the conclusion. Points are included after each choice. Minimum -2, maximum +2.

Favors and Enmity

The characters have the opportunity to earn the following during play.

Favor of Big Hill guards. You gave back the dead guard's necklace and armor, despite personal value. This earned the favor of his brothers. So long as you have this favor, all future Charisma (Deception, Intimidation, or Persuasion) made against gnomish guards are made with advantage.

Enmity of Big Hill guards. You told the guards the caves were clear, but they were not. The guards are distrustful of you. So long as you have this enmity, all future Charisma (Deception, Intimidation, or Persuasion) made against gnomish guards are made with disadvantage.

The Serpent's Gauntlet

The players will continue the Ranger's trials, sailing through the breadth of the Ice Mountains on their way to the Great Serpent in search of a sea elf. Along the way, they must face monsters of the frozen south, including the Ice Kraken, and when they get to the sea elves, they must complete a task set by the queen before they can continue to Aeun with their final companion.

Background

See session I background for previous information about the prophecy and Ranger trial, including the forest trial.

During the Gnome Session, the players head to the Big Hill, and Chief Sokti gives them the task of clearing out the Caves of Chittering Darkness, which was home to a nest of giant spiders. The party eliminates the spiderlings and egg sacs, defeats the giant spider mother, and rescues survivors. Having completed Chief Sokti's trial, the Ranger has earned a gnomish companion. Kip, a Big Hill guard, joins the group after his sister and nephew are rescued from the caves.

> Note: For the purpose of this game, you will have your full party from the moment Mara leaves the Gnome Lands. They won't meet people again until the Great Serpent.

The Ice Mountains

Once they are ready, the party sets sail from the Big Hill and toward the Ice Mountains. This journey takes months. Adjust accordingly.

> *The Ice Mountains. Perhaps it wasn't the most imaginative name, but it sure was accurate. The area was plain, cold, rugged, and wild. Decent creatures didn't live in the frozen south. All sorts of monsters like the ones Mara had read about in the monster manuals roamed ahead. There were frost giants, ice goblins, snowy golems, and winter wolves on land, and in water, serpents, polar piranha, winter whales, and, somewhere . . . an ice kraken . . . Their tentacles are more solid, with sharp ice shards on the back made to shred ships. . . . Its icy touch spreads and spreads. Anything it touches will be covered in a sheet of ice. And its final weapon is frost. When the kraken gets close enough for you to see its teeth, you're likely to die from its frosty breath. Like a dragon breathes fire, it breathes frost. Whatever that touches, you likely lose forever."*
>
> (*Ranger's Odyssey*, 113–114)

The monsters whose names began with winter exploded with wintry blast when injured. Just like the winter whale had burst frosty air at Mara, giving her frostbite and hitting her with her own axe, winter wolves would blast a wintry mix when injured.

Snowy monsters were actually created from the snow itself. The golem could appear out of nowhere, whisked up from harmless tundras. They were difficult to defeat because they were made of only snow. The only way to defeat the creature made completely of snow was to melt it, so—if they were unlucky enough to meet a golem—they would have to get the golem to the water so it would turn into a slushy puddle.

Frost monsters, like the giants, had armor of frost. Little ice crystals made their bodies a deathly blue. In order to injure them, they would have to pierce the armor. This is why the men had javelins—the javelin would drive through the frost and into its mark. Polar creatures, like the polar piranha, were the mildest of the ice monsters. They were white—to blend in with their surroundings—and they had powerful jaws with sharp teeth. The polar bears on Earth were likely named in this fashion.

The ice monsters were arguably the worst—and not just because one of them was the kraken. It was imperative to defeat them at a distance so they would be unable to use their frosty breath. Aside from this, the commonality with the ice monsters was their icy touch. The tentacles of the ice kraken would freeze whatever they touched. The water around the kraken turned to slush as it swam, and a swipe of the tentacle on the deck would leave an icy sheet where the tentacle had been—with a jagged edge out a foot or two wider than the tentacle itself. The ice goblins materialized icicle weapons. A cut from one of them would make Mara's current frostbite seem like nothing. In addition, their touch would leave an icy shell where their hand had been. On a person, this would be a frozen handprint. On the ground or other surfaces, the layer of ice would shoot out a foot or two like the tentacles of the kraken.

(*Ranger's Odyssey*, 128)

Note: In the book, the party faces a winter whale (page 123), polar piranhas (page 130–131), and then the ice kraken. Once they face the kraken, they go to land to repair the ship. They face a few monsters while aground before moving on. For the purpose of this session, some will be expanded or contracted, and some are out of order.

Not all elements in the book directly translate to D&D, but the creatures have been kept regardless of D&D challenge rating. It is important that you use the monster stats from this book rather than your standard 5e source to ensure that adjustments to difficulty are applied for your session.

This adventure begins with damage to the ship from icebergs. The party has to make an emergency docking in the Ice Mountains and fetch lumber to repair the ship before continuing their journey.

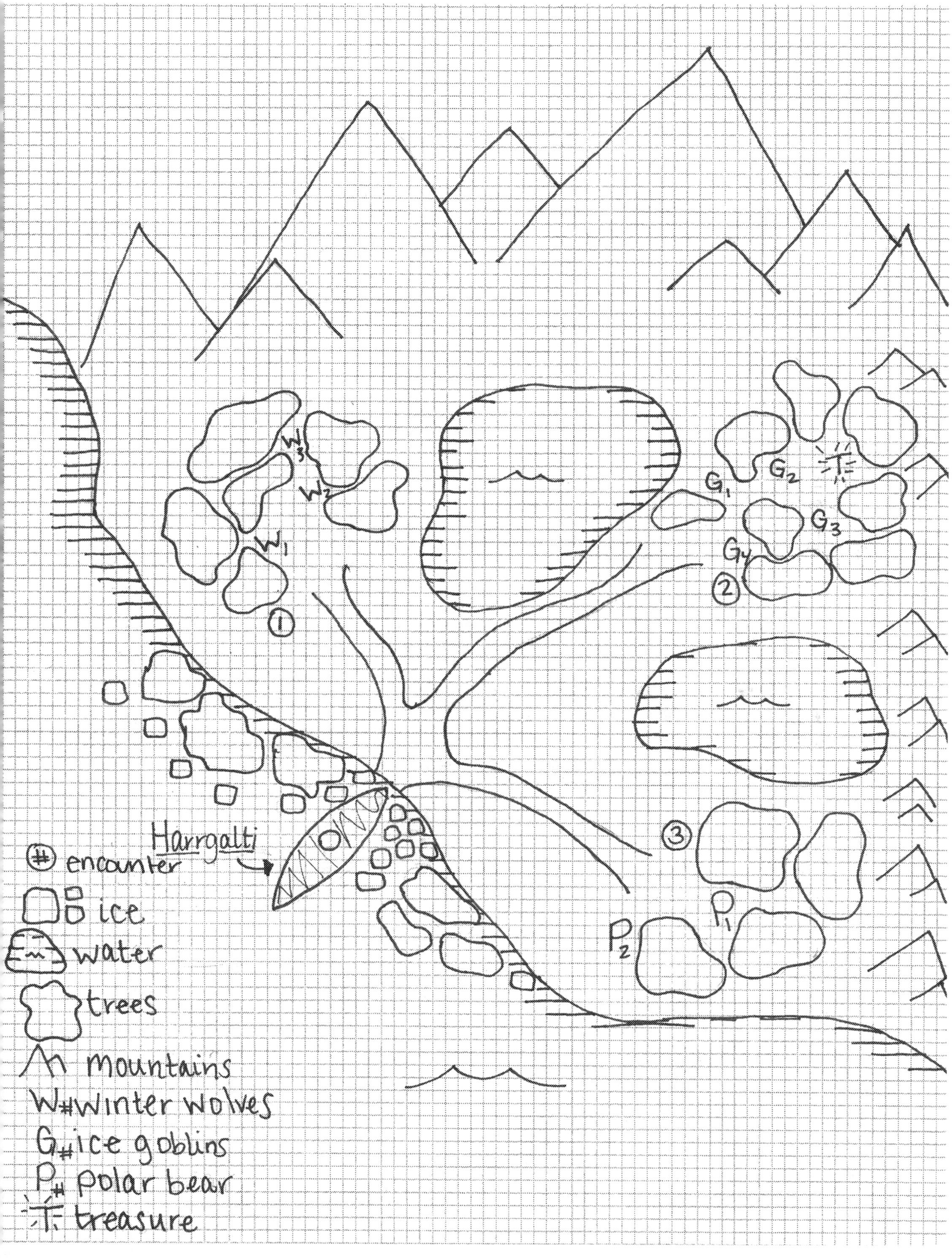
W3
W2
W1
1
G1
G2
T
G3
G4
2
Harrgalti
3
P1
P2
encounter
ice
water
trees
mountains
W# winter wolves
G# ice goblins
P# polar bear
T treasure

Part 1: Sea and Ice

Harrgalti comes to a stop in a collection of ice blocks on the way, because the person on watch can see trees on the landmass. There are three worn paths leading to three separate groves. The players must choose which path to take. Each path will take them to the lumber they need, and each path will result in an encounter. They can choose to take more than one path for the sake of XP, but they are only meant to pick one. If any players have a tracking ability, they can investigate tracks to determine their path.

There are winter clothes on the ship for player use, so there should not be ill effects from cold.

1: Winter Wolves

The party chooses the left path. Deep tracks in the snow lead all the way to the forest. They look like dog prints to an untrained eye, but a tracker could identify them as large wolf tracks (Investigation or Animal Handling DC 12). Players can turn back any time up to the edge of the treeline. If they begin to chop any wood or they enter the grove, the winter wolves will sniff them out. To get the necessary wood, they have to fight.

Winter Wolf

Large monstrosity, neutral evil
Armor Class 13 (natural armor)
Hit Points 50 (7d10 + 10)
Speed 50 ft.

STR	DEX	CON	INT	WIS	CHA
18 (+4)	13 (+1)	14 (+2)	7 (-2)	12 (+1)	8 (-1)

Skills Perception +5, Stealth +3
Damage Immunities cold
Senses passive Perception 15
Challenge 1 (200 XP)

Keen Hearing and Smell. The wolf has advantage on Wisdom (Perception) checks that rely on hearing or smell.
Pack Tactics. The wolf has advantage on an attack roll against a creature if at least one of the wolf's allies is within 5 feet of the creature and the ally isn't incapacitated.
Snow Camouflage. The wolf has advantage on Dexterity (Stealth) checks made to hide in snowy terrain.
Death Burst. When the wolf dies, it explodes in a burst of jagged ice. Each creature within 5 feet of it must make a DC 10 Dexterity saving throw, taking 4 (1d8) slashing damage on a failed save, or half as much damage on a successful one.

Actions

Bite. *Melee Weapon Attack*: +6 to hit, reach 5 ft., one target. *Hit*: 11 (2d6 + 4) piercing damage. If the target is a creature, it must succeed on a DC 14 Strength saving throw or be knocked prone.

Frost Breath (Recharge 6). The wolf exhales a 15-foot cone of cold air. Each creature in that area must succeed on a DC 10 Dexterity saving throw, taking 5 (2d4) cold damage on a failed save, or half as much damage on a successful one.
Arctic-dwelling winter wolves are evil and intelligent creatures with snow-white fur and pale blue eyes.

Note: Wolf 1 should be adjusted to half HP with Action limited to Bite.

Adjusting the Encounter: Winter wolves are numbered on the map.

—Very weak: use winter wolf 1.
—Weak: use winter wolf 2.
—Strong: use winter wolves 1 & 2.
—Very strong: use winter wolves 1–3.

The party can retreat if they are unable to defeat the wolves, and they can recuperate on the ship and try again. If they are successful in defeating the wolves, they will be able to repair the ship and continue on their way. Alternately, they can choose to take one of the other paths for further encounters.

2: Ice Goblins

The party chooses the center path. This path is the longest and requires the group to go between two large, frozen ponds. Deep tracks in the snow lead all the way to the forest. They're just boot tracks, but from small feet. That's all that may be discerned from them. (DC 10) Players can turn back any time up to the edge of the treeline. If they begin to chop any wood or they enter the grove, ice goblin scouts will spot them and attack. To get the necessary wood, they have to fight.

Ice Goblin

Small elemental humanoid (goblinoid), neutral evil
Armor Class 15 (leather armor, shield)
Hit Points 7 (2d6)
Speed 30 ft.

STR	DEX	CON	INT	WIS	CHA
7 (-2)	13 (+1)	10 (+0)	9 (-1)	11 (+0)	12 (+1)

Skills Perception +2, Stealth +3
Damage vulnerabilities bludgeoning, fire
Damage Immunities cold, poison
Condition Immunities poisoned
Senses darkvision 60 ft., passive Perception 12
Languages Common
Challenge 1/2 (100 XP)

Nimble Escape. The goblin can take the Disengage or Hide action as a bonus action on each of its turns.
Death Burst. When the goblin dies, it explodes in a burst of jagged ice. Each creature within 5 feet of it must make a DC 10 Dexterity saving throw, taking 4 (1d8) slashing damage on a failed save, or half as much damage on a successful one.
False Appearance. While the ice goblin remains motionless, it is indistinguishable from an ordinary block of ice.

Actions

Scimitar. *Melee Weapon Attack:* +4 to hit, reach 5 ft., one target. *Hit:* 5 (1d6 + 2) slashing damage.
Shortbow. *Ranged Weapon Attack:* +4 to hit, range 80/320 ft., one target. *Hit:* 5 (1d6 + 2) piercing damage.
Claws. *Melee Weapon Attack:* +3 to hit, reach 5 ft., one creature. *Hit:* 3 (1d4 + 1) slashing damage plus 2 (1d4) cold damage.

Frost Breath (Recharge 6). The goblin exhales a 15-foot cone of cold air. Each creature in that area must succeed on a DC 10 Dexterity saving throw, taking 5 (2d4) cold damage on a failed save, or half as much damage on a successful one.

Adjusting the Encounter: Ice goblins are numbered on the map.

—Very weak or weak: use ice goblins 1 & 2.
—Strong: use ice goblins 1–3.
—Very strong: use ice goblins 1–4.

Adjusting the Encounter: Ice goblins are numbered on the map.

—Very weak or weak: use ice goblins 1 & 2.
—Strong: use ice goblins 1–3.
—Very strong: use ice goblins 1–4.

The party can retreat if they are unable to defeat the ice goblins, and they can recuperate on the ship and try again. If they are successful in defeating the ice goblins, they will be able to repair the ship and continue on their way. Alternately, they can choose to take one of the other paths for further encounters.

Treasure

Whereas the wolves and bears have simple dens, the ice goblins live in a structure made of ice. It's a hut about the size of a kid's playhouse. If the players go inside, they will find two bottles of red liquid (potions of healing—2d4+2 HP) per player and a sapphire. Additionally, one ice goblin will drop a Frost Brand.

3: Polar Bears

Deep tracks in the snow lead all the way to the forest. They are very clearly tracks belonging to at least one large bear. (DC 10) The bears will spot them much earlier than the winter wolves or ice goblins. By the time they are halfway up the path, they will be spotted. To get the necessary wood, they have to fight.

Polar Bear

Large beast, unaligned
Armor Class 12 (natural armor)
Hit Points 42 (5d10 + 15)
Speed 40 ft., swim 30 ft

STR	DEX	CON	INT	WIS	CHA
20 (+5)	10 (+0)	16 (+3)	2 (-4)	13 (+1)	7 (-2)

Skills Perception +3
Damage Immunities cold
Senses passive Perception 13
Challenge 2 (450 XP)

Keen Smell. The bear has advantage on Wisdom (Perception) checks that rely on smell.

Actions
Multiattack. The bear makes two attacks: one with its bite and one with its claws.
Bite. *Melee Weapon Attack*: +7 to hit, reach 5 ft., one target. *Hit*: 9 (1d8 + 5) piercing damage.
Claws. *Melee Weapon Attack*: +7 to hit, reach 5 ft., one target. *Hit*: 12 (2d6 + 5) slashing damage.

Note: Polar Bear 1 should be adjusted to half HP with Action limited to Bite. No multiattack.

Adjusting the Encounter: Polar bears are numbered on the map.

—Very weak or weak: use polar bear 1.
—Weak: use polar bear 2.
—Strong: use polar bears 1 & 2.
—Very strong: use polar bears 1 & 2, both at full health and ability.

The party can retreat if they are unable to defeat the polar bears, but the polar bears will chase them back to the ship (and can then be taken out with missile weapons). If they are successful in defeating the polar bear(s), they will be able to repair the ship and continue on their way. Alternately, they can choose to take one of the other paths for further encounters.

Part 2: The Kraken

Once the ship was repaired, *Harrgalti* set off again across the southern edge of the mainland and made its way through the icy waters toward the Great Serpent.

After a few days at sea, during a night watch, the sea around the ship turned to slush. A chill that had nothing to do with the Ice Mountains whispered on the breeze, and a giant, mast-sized tentacle rose from the water and crashed onto the deck, shooting out a jagged layer of ice from the point of impact.

The full kraken encounter may be found on pages 134–136 of *Ranger's Odyssey*. In D&D, the kraken is a legendary beast that's way, *way* beyond the level of anyone who could go on this quest, but it is an important part of *Ranger's Odyssey*. The ice kraken stats have been leveled for this purpose, coming from a mixture of kraken and giant octopus, with the ice elements added.

Ice Kraken

Gargantuan monstrosity (titan), chaotic evil

Armor Class 16 (natural armor)
Hit Points 52 ((3d10+PC) + (2PC))
Speed 10 ft., swim 60 ft.

STR	DEX	CON	INT	WIS	CHA
17 (+3)	13 (+1)	13 (+1)	4 (-3)	10 (+0)	4 (-3)

Saving Throws Str +17, Dex +7, Con +14, Int +13, Wis +11
Damage Immunities lightning; bludgeoning, piercing, and slashing from nonmagical attacks, cold
Condition Immunities frightened, paralyzed
Senses truesight 120 ft., passive Perception 14
Challenge 3 (700 XP)

Amphibious. The kraken can breathe air and water.
Freedom of Movement. The kraken ignores difficult terrain, and magical effects can't reduce its speed or cause it to be restrained. It can spend 5 feet of movement to escape from nonmagical restraints or being grappled.
Underwater Camouflage. The kraken has advantage on Dexterity (Stealth) checks made while underwater.

Actions

Multiattack. The kraken makes two tentacle attacks.
Tentacles. *Melee Weapon Attack:* +5 to hit, reach 15 ft., one target. *Hit:* 10 (2d6 + 3) bludgeoning damage. If the target is a creature, it is grappled (escape DC 16). Until this grapple ends, the target is restrained, and the octopus can't use its tentacles on another target.

Icy Touch. When the kraken hits the tentacle on the ship, a layer of ice will spread in a splintered cone 10ft. Each creature in that area must succeed on a DC 10 Dexterity saving throw, taking 5 (2d4) cold damage on a failed save, or half as much damage on a successful one.

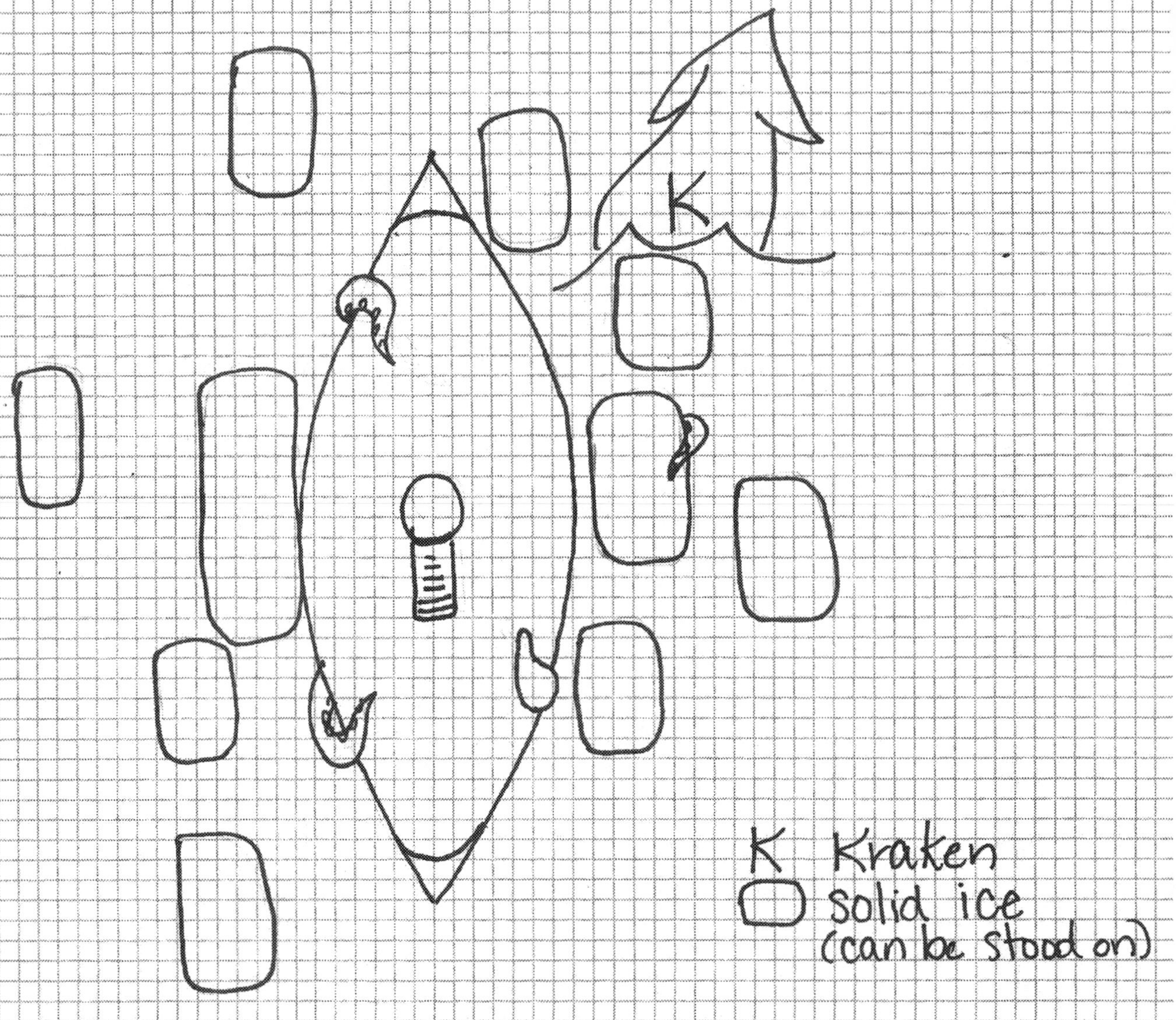
K
K Kraken
solid ice
(can be stood on)

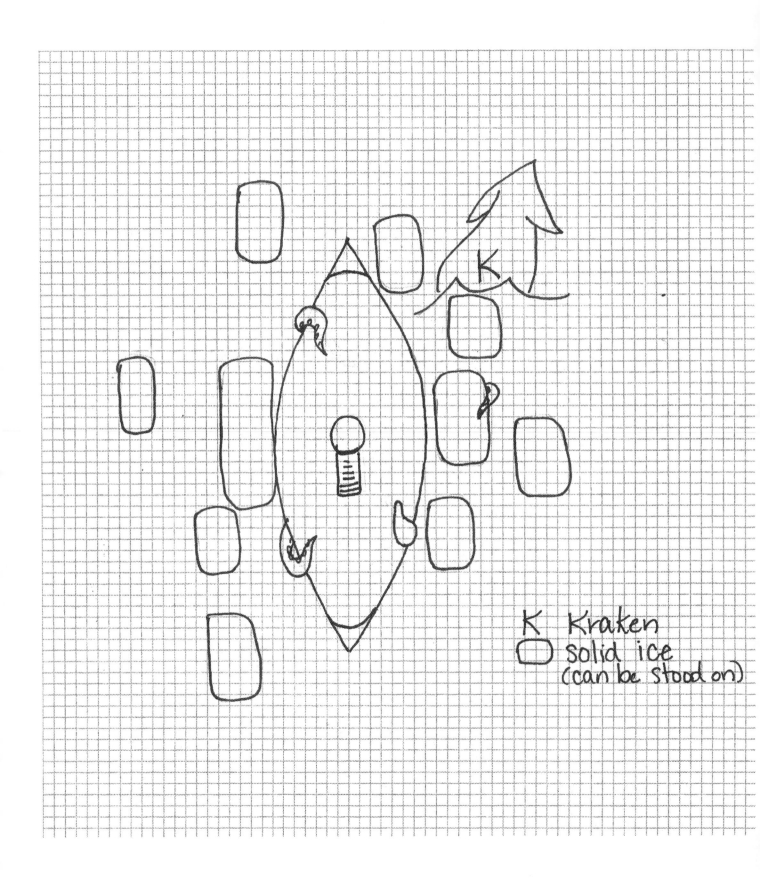

To accommodate all combat styles, players will be able to fight the kraken either by using missile weapons from the ship or melee weapons when the tentacles come within reach, or they may leave the ship and engage in close combat from solid patches of floating ice. As with the giant spider encounter in the Gnome Session, there is no leveling for this encounter.

Every 3 rounds, the kraken will slam another tentacle up on the deck, creating an ice hazard and requiring all party members fighting from the deck to make a saving throw to avoid impact or ice damage.

In the book, the kraken is defeated by one well-thrown javelin through the eye. Regardless of the final blow, when the kraken dies, it releases one final roar before sinking into the water and disappearing into the depths below.

The Sea Elves

There will be no treasure from the encounter, but a sea elf ship spotted the battle from a distance, and one of the crewmen on the ship, Finn, will recount the tale to those he meets. After using some of the lumber gathered in part I and other supplies below deck, they continue on their way toward the Great Serpent. However, it is not long before they are accosted by ships of sea elves.

> *The elven ships closed in on either side of* Harrgalti. *The crews lined the edges of their ships closest to the intruders. With a lurch, Mara noticed they all carried sharp spears like harpoons. Like the ships, the elves themselves were all the colors of the sea. . . . the elves had varying shades of greens and blues—seafoam green, ocean blue, seaweed green, ocean mist blue. Their hair complimented their skin, also in varying sea greens and blues—but what stood out the most to Mara was how fierce they looked. . . . The sea elves on both ships began rhythmically pounding the butts of their harpoons on the deck.*
>
> (*Ranger's Odyssey*, 143)

At this point, the players will have three choices:

1. They can surrender to the sea elves and be brought before the queen.
2. They can explain themselves honestly and be brought before the queen.
3. They can try to fight, be overcome with no encounter, and be brought before the queen.

The only difference here is the XP. The correct response is to stand up to them without fighting, explaining to the sea elves that they alone were able to defeat the kraken and have earned an audience with the queen. The sea elves take them to their islands.

Part 3: The Gauntlet

The party is hauled around the Great Serpent to the Crown, the capitol of the sea elves' islands, and they are taken by guards onto the docks and up to the queen's castle for an audience.

> *The sea elves were clearly a marine-centered society. All buildings and decorations were made of objects from the sea. . . .*
>
> *The people themselves were naturally colors of the sea. Beyond that, they wore spiked knee-high boots that appeared to be made of fish scales. Rather than pants, they wore strange, tight shorts. The material glistened—reminding Mara of something surfers or scuba divers would wear. Around their torsos, they wore tunics of brightly colored chainmail. From watching a blacksmith at a festival, Mara realized the effect of blues and purples in the metal was achieved by scorching in the forge. There appeared to be something like swim shirts underneath. Looped into the shoulder of the chainmail were large shells that were used like shoulder pads. Most of the elves had long hair, partially knotted or braided to pull it back out of their faces. Some of them had pulled the small knots or braids into a large, high ponytail.*
>
> *. . . the figure on the coral flag was a sea monster. Fitting. They passed under a high arch and followed a flight of stairs into the castle. Down a few twisting hallways, they stopped in front of two burly guards in front of a coral-colored door. When they arrived, the guards pounded their spears on the ground three times and opened the door.*
>
> *They stepped into a large hall—a classic throne room. Sitting on a magnificent sea throne was a beautiful blue elf with coral pink hair matching the other coral Mara had seen. Her hair was braided and curled, looping around a yellow coral crown. There were guards on either side of the throne. Behind the throne, a woman stood on the left. She had seafoam green skin and short, spiked, deep blue hair. One hand was on her sword's hilt. To the right of the throne was a young man with blue skin and bright green hair.* (*Ranger's Odyssey*, 144–145)

This is the point when the characters meet Finn, the intended companion on their journey. Their choices in the rest of the session will determine if Finn actually joins them. First, they have to deal with Queen Ula.

> **Queen Ula as an NPC:** Sitting on a magnificent sea throne was a beautiful blue elf with coral pink hair matching the other coral Mara had seen. Her hair was braided and curled, looping around a yellow coral crown. She is haughty and cold.

For the purpose of the session, some of this trial has been eliminated and replaced with rest areas for the players, so there are fewer challenges to face. If the DM would like to include those, refer to the book.

The Sea Trial

Queen Ula calls the party to the hall and informs them that in order to earn their sea elf companion—and to even survive the Great Serpent, they must prove their worth to the sea elves.

> *"In order to earn our expertise, you have to prove that you possess the courage we prize. Tomorrow, you must prove yourself to us beyond all doubt. . . . In the morning, you will be summoned for the Serpent's Gauntlet." . . . "The Serpent's Gauntlet will test you according to the standards of my*

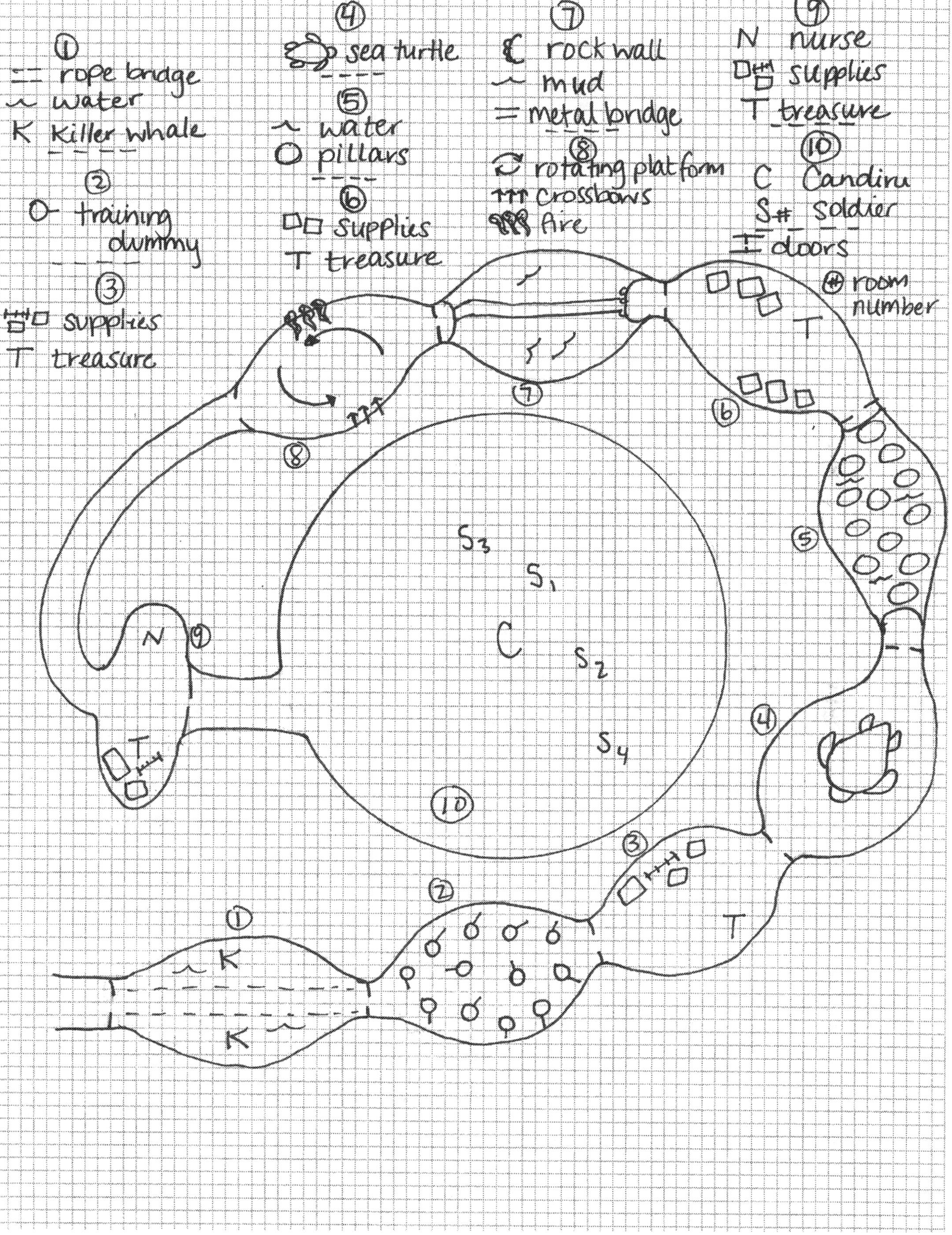

1
rope bridge
water
K Killer whale
2
training dummy
3
supplies
T treasure
4
sea turtle
5
water
pillars
6
supplies
T treasure
7
rock wall
mud
metal bridge
8
rotating platform
crossbows
fire
9
N nurse
supplies
T treasure
10
C Candiru
S# soldier
doors
room number
K
K
T
N
S_3
S_1
C
S_2
S_4
T
T

people. You will complete a series of physical tests to determine your skill, your resilience, and your courage. If you complete the gauntlet, your final test will be to defeat [Candiru, the woman who stands by the throne] . . . If you are able to complete my gauntlet tomorrow and defeat Candiru in battle, you will have earned the right to remain on our island and I will allow someone to accompany you to complete your trial." (*Ranger's Odyssey*, 151)

> NOTE: For the purpose of this adventure, no player characters have any advantages or knowledge to use in the gauntlet, even if the PC is a sea elf.

The gauntlet is set up like a dungeon in an arena. A map is included with a modified gauntlet, taking a collection of the areas and translating them to the game, replacing others with supply rooms. At the DM's discretion, the eliminated areas could instead be added back in. For the full gauntlet, see *Ranger's Odyssey* Chapter 15: The Gauntlet (pages 158–173).

> NOTE: When entering the gauntlet, the players are allowed only one melee weapon and no tools or packs. Players must select weapons before entering and are led through a tunnel when ready.

There are double doors closed at the end of the tunnel, and they are given directions. "Once you enter those doors, you will be sealed into the gauntlet. You will not leave unless you make it through all ten stages. Your time does not matter, only your completion. The gauntlet can sometimes last all morning or all day. Step up to the doors. Once the bell sounds again, your trial will begin." (*Ranger's Odyssey*, 158)

General Features

Rooms are numbered on the map. There is only one path through the gauntlet. Players must complete all ten rooms in order.

Ceilings and Walls. There is no ceiling. The whole area is open so spectators can view the gauntlet from stands around it. The walls to each area are 15 foot high, made of stone, and the areas are connected by double doors. The walled gauntlet is set up in an arena reminiscent of the Roman Coliseum.

Light. It is daylight when the players begin the gauntlet. It should remain so for the duration.

Sound. As the stands are full of spectators, the players can hear spectator reactions as they play. If they take too long to do something, the audience will boo them. Actions they make will be met with audible reactions.

1: Killer Whales

The bell sounds, indicating that the gauntlet has officially begun, and the doors open to allow the players to enter the first area. From the book:

She stood on a small platform facing a strange canopy. There were six poles standing over a large pool. Spanning the tops of the six poles was a large net that appeared to be the rigging from a ship. Finn had told her that, for this first area, she had to cross the pool without getting in the water. It was a significant distance to try to cross—probably around fifty feet.

With a deep breath, Mara stepped forward and looked down into the pool. (*Ranger's Odyssey*, 159)

For this session, much is the same. However, instead of netting to scale, the players see a rickety rope bridge. They must cross the rope bridge to get to the door on the other side, but when they look into the water from the platform, they can see two large killer whales swimming in the water below.

> NOTE: In the book, there are sharks in this pool, and it is deeper. DM may replace the killer whales with a type of shark or whale instead.

Killer Whale

Huge beast, unaligned
Armor Class 12 (natural armor)
Hit Points 90 (12d12 + 12)
Speed swim 60 ft.

STR	DEX	CON	INT	WIS	CHA
19 (+4)	10 (+0)	13 (+1)	3 (-4)	12 (+1)	7 (-2)

Skills Perception +3
Senses blindsight 120 ft., passive Perception 13
Challenge 3 (700 XP)

Echolocation. The whale can't use its blindsight while deafened.
Hold Breath. The whale can hold its breath for 30 minutes.
Keen Hearing. The whale has advantage on Wisdom (Perception) checks that rely on hearing.

Actions

Bite. *Melee Weapon Attack:* +6 to hit, reach 5 ft., one target. *Hit:* 21 (5d6 + 4) piercing damage.

Traversing this room with care will allow them to reach the door without combat. They cannot speak to the whales, but if they cross the bridge without reacting to the whales below them, they can make it to the other side. About every 10 feet walked, one of the whales will bump the rope bridge.

> Each time, all players on the bridge roll their d00/d%. 40 and above, and they stay on the bridge. 10–30, and they fall into the water. (70% chance to stay.)

If a player falls into the water, the party must fight. The water is only about 5 foot deep, so many players can stand up and fight in it (if their party doesn't take immediate action to get them out of the water). The whales will fight at a disadvantage due to the depth.

When all players make it across the bridge, this area is complete. There is a click, and a net raises from the water to keep the whales away from the platform.

2: Training Dummies

When the players enter the next area, they find that they are faced with a whole room of wooden, mechanical training dummies. Unlike typical dummies that would take momentum from the trainee to move, these are moved by cranks at the bases, operated by sea elves below. They do not stop.

Once the door opened, there was another click, and the figures in the room began to move. The whole room ahead of her was filled with rotating posts. Each post had an arm or two sticking out the side and metal spikes covering its entire surface.

Mara glared at the obstacles ahead of her, trying to find some sort of pattern. She could see to the left, there seemed to be a little more space. She might be able to make it through there. Jumping in place for a moment to prepare herself, Mara moved to the left and stepped in between two posts.

She was immediately winded as one arm hit her in the stomach. It bounced her off into another post, which swept her back out of the field again.
(*Ranger's Odyssey*, 162)

Attempting to power through the room will result in a similar encounter. Players must figure out another way through.

OPTIONS:

—Players can fight enough dummies to make a path. They attack on a pattern. Each dummy has a AC 15 and hp 15, and there are 12 total dummies. Destroying 4 dummies will create a path. Being hit will result in 1d4+2 bludgeoning damage.
—Players with at least DC 15 Athletics (Str), Acrobatics (Dex), or Investigation (Int) saving throw may attempt to discern the pattern and walk through.
—DM may offer players another option, depending on player abilities.

Once players reach the platform by the far door, there will be another clicking sound, and all the dummies will stop moving.

3: SUPPLY STOP I

Rather than another puzzle, this room holds supplies for the players to aid them in continuing through the gauntlet. If the DM chooses, this room could instead be placed with a low-level encounter or the jellyfish room from the book.

Supplies:

—1 potion of healing per player (2d4+2 HP)
—bandages

There is no time limit here, so whenever the players are ready, they can leave the room to proceed to the next. If any players have lost their weapons for any reason, there will also be enough here to put them back to the level they started.

4: GIANT SEA TURTLE

When the players are ready to continue, they will proceed to the fourth room.

This room was different. It seemed still and calm. There were a few mossy rocks to one side, a small bank to the other, and a shallow pool in the center. Resting halfway out of this shallow pool was a giant sea turtle with a face more like that of a snapping turtle.
(*Ranger's Odyssey*, 166)

The key here is honesty. The giant sea turtle can speak Common, but he will wait to see what the players do first. If the players try to fight without talking to him, he will fight to the death. If they speak to him and lie, the same will occur. Killing the sea turtle has no negative effects (though the spectators will boo).

GIANT TURTLE

Huge beast, unaligned
Armor Class 11
Hit Points 52 (8d10 + 8)
Speed 10 ft., swim 60 ft.

STR	DEX	CON	INT	WIS	CHA
17 (+3)	13 (+1)	13 (+1)	4 (-3)	10 (+0)	4 (-3)

Skills Perception +4, Stealth +5
Senses darkvision 60 ft., passive Perception 14
Challenge 1 (200 XP)

Keen Hearing. The turtle has advantage on Wisdom (Perception) checks that rely on hearing.

ACTIONS

Bite. *Melee Weapon Attack:* +6 to hit, reach 5 ft., one target. *Hit:* 21 (3d6) piercing damage.

If the players simply answer the turtle honestly, they will be allowed to pass without combat. If they answer honestly and treat the sea turtle with respect, he will give them a clue for Room 8. Players should not be told that it's a clue, just a fact from the turtle.

The first question is a matter of opinion. Players just have to give their honest opinion and not just say "sea turtles" because that's what they think he wants to hear.

Questions <u>each player</u> must answer honestly:

—What is the greatest creature of the sea?
—Why are you completing the gauntlet?

Clue if <u>all players</u> are respectful:

—The treasure of the sea is a mermaid, known as the Angel of the Sea to the sea elves.

Once the characters have either received the sea turtle's approval or defeated him in battle, the door behind him will unlock, and they can proceed.

5: Pillars

The door out of this room is up high, and reaching the end requires the players to climb.

> *The fifth area was a room full of stone pillars at varying heights. Finn had told her she would not make it to the end unless she moved quickly. The pillars themselves were sticking out of steaming, bubbling water. Boiling. She would have to cross the room without falling into the water. Peering across, she couldn't see a doorway. Mara looked all over the room before finally seeing an opening near the top of the wall on the opposite side.*
>
> *The first two pillars stood in front of her like stepping stones. Not wanting to wait, since Finn had said this area was all about speed, Mara stepped onto the first pillar. Nothing happened. Encouraged, she stepped forward to the next pillar. This one began to rumble and sink into the water as she stood.*
>
> (*Ranger's Odyssey*, 164)

Each pillar only has enough space for one player to stand on it at a time. Weight doesn't make the pillars sink faster, but they are triggered to begin sinking by someone standing on them. They will not sink completely into the water, but they will sink right up to it. If all the players try to go at once, only the first will be able to make it to the platform unless they took different paths.

If another tries to jump to the platform in the same run from the same pillar, they will need to successfully complete a DC 10 Acrobatics (Dex) saving throw to safely fall back onto the pillar. They cannot make the jump. Failing the throw will just incur fall damage (1d6). Then, all players who didn't make it across have to walk back to the beginning, rolling 1d4 every jump to see if they are splashed by the boiling water that will then be close to them.

Once all the pillars are vacant, they will rise back to their full height, resetting for the next run. Once all players have crossed, the door will unlock.

6: Supply Stop II

Rather than another puzzle, this room holds supplies for the players to aid them in continuing through the gauntlet. If the DM chooses, this room could instead be placed with a low-level encounter or the kraken room from the book.

Note: If using the kraken room, be sure to have the killing blow in Part II be the kraken's eye or change it to match your plans here—it just needs to match.

Supplies:

—1 potion of healing per player (2d4+2 HP)
—bandages

There is no time limit here, so whenever the players are ready, they can leave the room to proceed to the next. If any players have lost their weapons for any reason, there will also be enough here to put them back to the level they started.

7: The Rock Wall

Through the next door, there is a harsh drop-off. If any players rush the door, they will need to complete a saving throw to avoid falling to 1d6 damage. At this point, they will be caught or catch themselves before falling to the ground.

> *Looking out into the next room, she discovered she was on a rock-climbing wall. Once she stepped off the small platform for the doorway, she would have to descend a rock wall. The footholds appeared to be made of different colors of coral—pink, blue, and yellow. Directly below her and out halfway through the room were spikes. She could see a thin pole crossing the sea of spikes. Beyond the pole, before the doorway, was a mud pit.*
>
> *For this room, Finn had told Mara to remember who the queen was and to not try the easy way—though the way was easy near the end.*
>
> (*Ranger's Odyssey*, 165)

Players can only use the pink holds to scale the rock wall. Blue and yellow ones will fall. Pink is the color of the queen's hair—only the queen's.

Player missteps have high chance of death. 1d6+2 piercing damage if they jump and fall on the spikes. Jumping to the mud will result in 1d6 + 2 bludgeoning damage, because it is only a foot deep. Players must scale the rock wall and cross the pole to avoid the spikes. Then, they just need to slog through the mud to the platform, and the door will unlock.

8: The Angel of the Sea

The players walk through the door and into a large room. Some mechanism makes the room dark while still allowing the spectators to see what's going on.

> *The next room Mara entered appeared to be empty. There were three other doors—one on each wall. An inscription on the floor read,* **The angel of the sea will set you free. . . .**
>
> *She looked around at the doors. The whole room was dark. She stepped into the room, and as her feet left the platform, the door behind swung shut. As soon as the door closed, the room was filled with sounds. All sorts of animal sounds erupted from each door. After playing all at once, the doors played one at a time.*
>
> (*Ranger's Odyssey*, 168)

When the players enter the room, they are able to view the inscription on the floor before the door behind them closes, and the room spins. All sorts of animal sounds play at once. There is silence for a moment. Then one sound will play at a time from one door.

The players have to select the correct door to safely leave the room. There is a pattern. Each round, a different animal will call. At the end of the round, there will be a click, and the room will spin again. The players will have a choice to open one of the doors or wait 20 seconds for another rotation and a different animal sound.

If the players showed respect to the giant sea turtle in Room 4, they were told that the Angel of the Sea is a mermaid. This should tell them that the mermaid's song is the correct sound. Others should be avoided.

Doors: Roll 1d4.

1. Room 7: Players can see back to the previous room.
2. Crossbows: If players open the door head-on, whoever stands in the doorway will receive 1d8+1 piercing damage. They reload each round.
3. Flamethrowers: If players open the door head-on, whoever stands in the doorway will receive 1d4+1 fire damage. These are replenished every round.
4. Room 9: Players will see a long hallway. There will be a click and the rooms will no longer spin.

If a 4 is rolled, the mermaid song will sound and the d6 roll (below) should be disregarded. Be sure to still roll both either way so the players are not tipped off to the success of the d4. If players don't open the door during this round, they will have to wait for the mermaid song again.

Otherwise—if the d4 does not result in a 4, the d6 will determine the sound that will play. The DM can describe or mimic sounds or prepare audio files ahead of time.

Animal sounds: Roll 1d6

1. Whale song
2. Seals
3. Walrus
4. Sea lions
5. Dolphins
6. Kraken

Players will remain in this room until they have selected the correct door. Once they open the door to Room 9, everything will stop, and they will walk down a long, curved hallway.

9: Rest Area

Players have all wounds tended and are able to rest and recuperate before heading into the final battle.

> *The ninth area was different. There was a round room with a couch, a table with food, a weapons rack, an armor rack, and, to one side, a cabinet, counter, and a chair in which an elderly blue-skinned woman sat. . . .*
>
> *The old woman tapped her throat silently and pointed to a sign on the wall to Mara's left.* You have thirty minutes in this room to rest before the arena. Allow the crone to attend to your wounds, eat a snack, change to dry armor, and select your weapons for the final challenge. (*Ranger's Odyssey*, 169)

Note: This counts as a short rest.

Players will use their standard melee weapons. Missile weapons are not permitted. However, if there has been any damage or loss of a weapon, the player may replace it here. If any players have been injured, their hit points will return to one below maximum without the use of any of their potions. When they are ready, they will proceed to the final area. There will be a countdown from ten—identified by a bell sounding—and the door will open.

10: Facing the Champion

The final room is a battle with the queen's champion, Candiru, and perhaps additional soldiers, depending on party strength. **Remember, no missile weapons!**

> *The bell sounded again. She opened the door and stepped out into the light of the open arena. The arena was simple—just a dirt circle with high walls. There was nothing else in the arena but the ferocious Candiru. Mara expected some kind of bell to signal the start, but Candiru's battle cry told her that was not the case.* (*Ranger's Odyssey*, 171)

Candiru

Medium humanoid (sea elf), neutral
Armor Class 16 (chain shirt, shield)
Hit Points 65 (10d8 + 20)
Speed 30 ft.

STR	DEX	CON	INT	WIS	CHA
15 (+2)	13 (+1)	14 (+2)	10 (+0)	12 (+1)	10 (+0)

Saving Throws Con +4, Str +4, Dex +5, Wis +2
Skills Athletics +4, Perception +4
Senses passive Perception 10
Languages Common, plus one of your choice
Challenge 2 (450 XP)

Second Wind. The warrior can use a bonus action on its turn to regain hit points equal to 1d10 + its level. If it does so, it can't use this feature again until it finishes a short or long rest.

Actions

Multiattack. The captain makes three melee attacks: two with its scimitar and one with its dagger. Or the captain makes two ranged attacks with its daggers

Longsword. *Melee Weapon Attack:* +4 to hit, reach 5 ft., one target. *Hit:* 6 (1d8 + 2) slashing damage, or 7 (1d10 + 2) slashing damage if used with two hands.

Dagger. *Melee or Ranged Weapon Attack:* +5 to hit, reach 5 ft. or range 20/60 ft., one target. Hit: 5 (1d4 + 3) piercing damage.

Reactions

Parry. The captain adds 2 to its AC against one melee attack that would hit it. To do so, the captain must see the attacker and be wielding a melee weapon.

Candiru as an NPC: She has seafoam green skin and short, spiked, deep blue hair. She is gruff and cocky. She's angry to be subjected to fighting who she considers untried adventurers.

Adjusting the Encounter: Preliminary soldiers are numbered on the map. Very weak parties will face Candiru only. For others, add 1 soldier per PC.

Once Candiru has been defeated, the players will have the choice to kill her or spare her.

◈ Sea Soldier

Medium humanoid (sea elf), neutral
Armor Class 16 (chain shirt, shield)
Hit Points 11 (2d8 + 2)
Speed 30 ft.

STR	DEX	CON	INT	WIS	CHA
11 (+0)	12 (+1)	12 (+1)	10 (+0)	10 (+0)	10 (+0)

Saving Throws Con +4
Skills Athletics +4, Perception +3, Survival +3
Senses passive Perception 10
Languages Common
Challenge 1/8 (25 XP)

Actions

Longsword. *Melee Weapon Attack*: +4 to hit, reach 5 ft., one target. *Hit*: 6 (1d8 + 2) slashing damage, or 7 (1d10 + 2) slashing damage if used with two hands.

Conclusion

If the players choose to kill Candiru, Ula is satisfied, and she selects someone to come with them on their journey. If the players choose to spare Candiru, the queen considers the run through the gauntlet to be a fail, and she refuses to give them someone for their journey—as they leave, Finn comes to speak to them.

> *"You failed the queen's gauntlet—but that wasn't where you needed to succeed," said Teddy. "Your trial is to undertake a predetermined task to earn your companion on the trial. You don't need the queen's approval—you need the companion's approval. If I'm not mistaken, Finn gave his approval when he helped you to prepare for the gauntlet." He turned to Finn. "Right?"*
>
> *"Mostly," Finn began. "I'd wanted to help you fight the kraken. When my mother declared the gauntlet was your trial, I had to see how that would end. And, well, where my mother saw you sparing Candiru as a weakness, I see it as a strength."*
>
> (*Ranger's Odyssey*, 176–177)

Having successfully earned their sea elf companion, the Ranger and party set sail for the rest of their journey together.

Rewards

Make sure if these characters will be played again that rewards are noted on player logsheets. In addition to the below standards rewards, as a story reward, the party has earned Finn as a party member.

Experience

Total all combat experience earned for defeated foes and divide by the number of characters present and surviving the combat. Non-combat experience should be counted by character. All players receive **400 base XP.**

200 + [non-combat] + ([combat] ÷ [party members])

Combat

Name of Foe	XP per Foe
Winter wolf	200
Ice goblin	100
Polar bear	450
Ice kraken	700
Killer whale	700
Giant sea turtle	200
Sea soldier	25
Candiru	450

Non-Combat

Task or Accomplishment	XP per Character
Find goblin treasure	25
Tell sea elves the truth	100
Don't fight killer whales	50
Figured out dummies<3rd try	50
Don't fight sea turtle	50
Figured out pillars <3rd try	50
Used pink coral by 2nd try	25
No more than 2 wrong doors	100
Spared Candiru	100

Treasure

Depending on the successful perception of all treasure caches, the players receive some or all of the below treasure. Characters should attempt to divide treasure evenly or by need wherever possible. If group is unable to decide, DM may select randomly.

Treasure	GP Value
Sapphire from goblins	1000
Potions of healing (2ea)—Goblins	50
Frost Brand	500
Potions of healing (2ea)—Gauntlet	50
Bandages	10

Renown

The players each earn one renown point for defeating the ice kraken. The gauntlet does not earn further renown.

Favors and Enmity

The characters have the opportunity to earn the following during play.

Favor of Sea elves. You killed Candiru even though you didn't need to. As a ruthless act, this has earned the favor of the sea elves. So long as you have this favor, all future Charisma (Deception, Intimidation, or Persuasion) made against any sea elves are made with advantage.

Enmity of Sea elves. You spared Candiru because she had been defeated, and killing someone just doing her duty is a waste. The sea elves view this as weakness and thus view you as weak. So long as you have this enmity, all future Charisma (Deception, Intimidation, or Persuasion) made against sea elves are made with disadvantage.

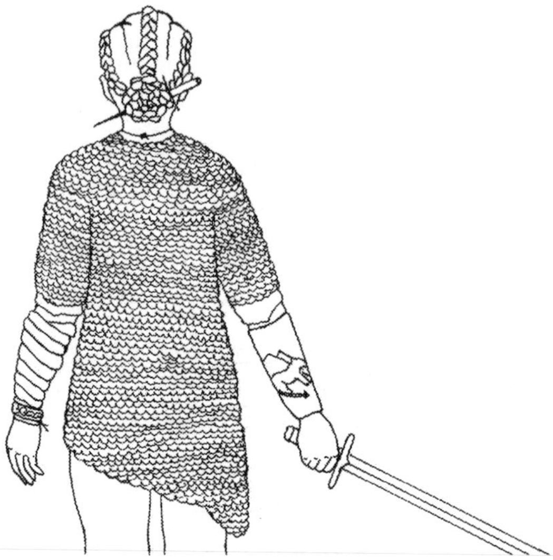

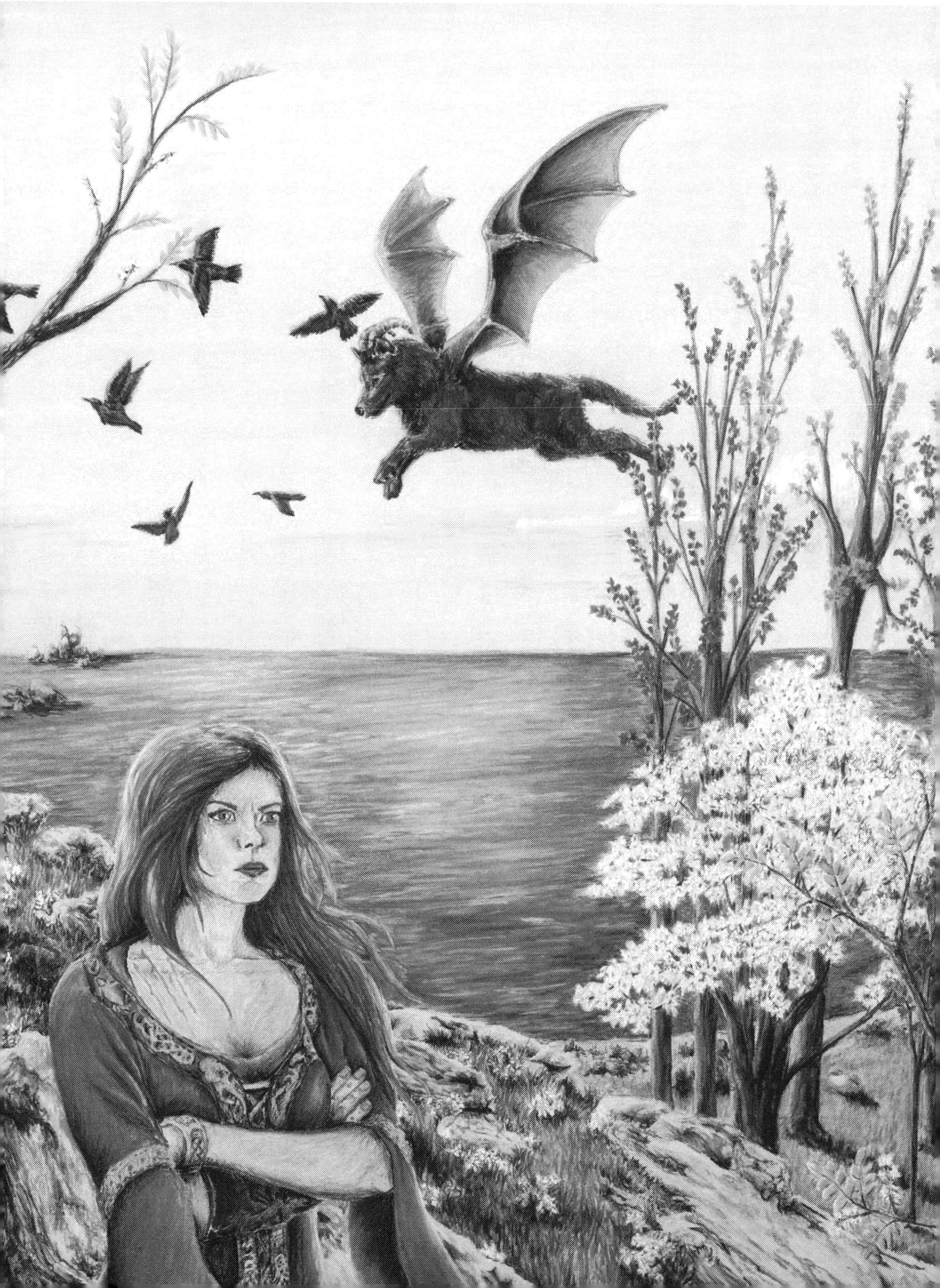

The Trickster and The Badger

Ranger's Odyssey follows a young woman named Mara as she undergoes preparations for her Ranger trial, earning the three companions she needs to complete a quest that will be set for her by the goddess. But every Ranger trial is different.

Mara's father, Toren, completed his own trial in his youth. His trial had a great impact on his people and the human village of Modoc, and it required the rangerling to enter Paeor's game and defeat the Trickster God of Ambergrove.

Background

As Mara ascends the steps of the village tree to meet with the Oracle and learn what her Ranger trial will be, her uncle Teddy tells her about her father, the Badger, and what he had to undergo to complete his own trial.

> *"For his trial, your dad had to find a human companion and travel deep into the earth near Modoc—a human town—to complete Paeor's game. Paeor is our trickster god. His game involved luring children and young warriors deep into the earth to a series of traps, beyond which was meant to be a treasure that would grant all of their greatest wishes."*
>
> *"He sounds like a fun guy," Mara said wryly.*
>
> *"Oh, yes, it goes just about as well as you'd think. According to the Oracle, a clear-headed human and a young Ranger would be able to find the traps and the right way through the deep, and finally be able to outwit the trickster and free the innocent. . . ."*
>
> (*Ranger's Odyssey*, 33)

Toren didn't have the luxury of taking his uncle Teddy, like Mara did. He couldn't take someone he trusted so completely, but when he went to Modoc, he found people more than willing to help.

As Mara's grandmother, Inola, tells her later in *Ranger's Odyssey*—

> *"The first thing he wanted to do to protect the people in the village was to get them to evacuate. He wanted them to move to a safer town." . . .*
>
> *"If he had been successful in convincing the people to evacuate, he would have failed his trial. He had to save the village as it was, not the people as they could be somewhere else. But . . . he wanted to make sure we were out of harm's way before he faced a god, and he was willing to fail his trial to ensure we survived." . . .*
>
> *"My lifemate and I decided to come here and to bring with us however many villagers wanted to go. The village split in half one day, and we packed up for the new life Toren made for us—but my lifemate had one more thing left to do before he would join us here." . . .*

The woman took a deep breath, steadying herself. "He volunteered to help Toren complete his trial by going with him into the lair and facing the traps . . ."
(*Ranger's Odyssey*, 188)

The human, Dakota, agreed to be Toren's companion as he faced Paeor's game. He must complete the game and save the existing village to earn the title of Ranger. Toren and his new companion make necessary preparations to face Paeor as part of the village evacuates and heads north to build Nimeda. With last goodbyes—Toren to Teddy and Dakota to Inola and their daughter, Kenda—the pair strode into the forest and to the maw of the trickster's game.

OPTIONAL: For the purpose of this session, the game does not need to be restricted to two players, and the sacrifice of the Ranger trial need not be included. It has been omitted from the materials, but the DM may choose to restore it. See Teddy's explanation in full on page 33.

Paeor's Game

The full session takes place within Paeor's game. Players will go into the game with the standard supplies on the character sheet. Although Toren does not take a rogue in the book, it is recommended that a rogue be included in a larger party.

General Features

Rooms are numbered on the map. There is only one way to go to make it through the game. This has been simplified for the purpose of this session. Players do not need to follow the story to complete the session, and it is not detailed in the book.

Ceilings and Walls. Once the players have entered the second area, everything is artistically masterful. 20-foot walls are made of solid marble, accented with pillars and carvings of the great Paeor. The pathways in Room 2 are about 8 foot wide. All the ceilings are at least 25 foot and vaulted.

Light. Torches line the pathways, and giant chandeliers lit with eternally burning candles hang every 15 feet along the peak.

Sound. The sounds of the dead echo throughout the entire game. Fancy as it appears, there is decay around every turn. The cackles and crackling of bone, the shuffling of footsteps, and the clanging of metal bounce around the perfect acoustics of the cathedral-like halls.

Traps. There are a total of 5 traps; 3 are in the main pathway, and 2 are in wrong turns in the labyrinth. These may be personalized by the DM or randomized based on common traps. All traps are intended to slow the players down, not kill them, so the included traps are simplified.

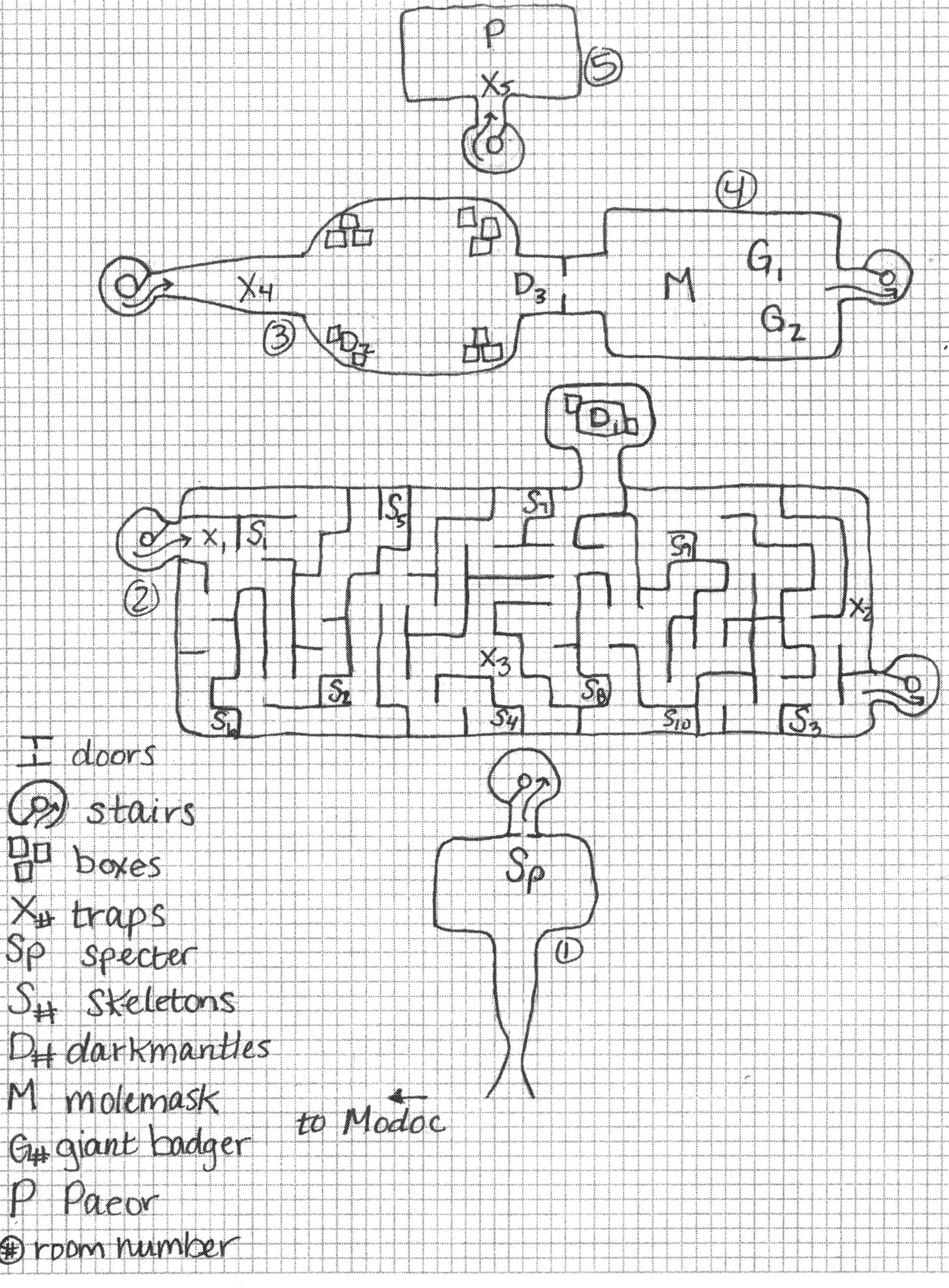
P
X5
5
4
G1
M
D3
X4
3
D2
G2
D1
S5
S7
S1
X1
S9
2
X2
X3
S2
S8
S6
S4
S10
S3
Sp
1
to Modoc
doors
stairs
boxes
X# traps
Sp specter
S# skeletons
D# darkmantles
M molemask
G# giant badger
P Paeor
room number

Once the players enter the opening of the game, there is no leaving alive unless they complete it.

1: Specter's Warning

The first room of the game appears like a standard cave. One lone torch is bolted to the wall at the back of the entrance, and glowing, amber letters appear on a stone door at the center of the back wall.

> Beyond Lies Paeor's Game
>
> *The Trickster invites you to test your mettle through the challenges in his game. Whosoever survives the game will be rewarded with a treasure beyond their wildest dreams.*

As the players examine the room and read the wall, a cackle meets their ears, and a spectral face emerges from behind the door.

Specter

Medium undead, chaotic evil (for this, unaligned)

Armor Class 12

Hit Points 22 (5d8)

Speed 0 ft., fly 50 ft. (hover)

STR	DEX	CON	INT	WIS	CHA
1 (-5)	14 (+2)	11 (+0)	10 (+0)	10 (+0)	11 (+0)

Damage Resistances acid, cold, fire, lightning, thunder; bludgeoning, piercing, and slashing from nonmagical attacks

Damage Immunities necrotic, poison

Condition Immunities charmed, exhaustion, grappled, paralyzed, petrified, poisoned, prone, restrained, unconscious

Senses darkvision 60 ft., passive Perception 10

Languages understands the languages it knew in life but can't speak

Challenge 1 (200 XP)

Incorporeal Movement. The specter can move through other creatures and objects as if they were difficult terrain. It takes 5 (1d10) force damage if it ends its turn inside an object.

Sunlight Sensitivity. While in sunlight, the specter has disadvantage on attack rolls, as well as on Wisdom (Perception) checks that rely on sight.

Actions

Life Drain. *Melee Spell Attack*: +4 to hit, reach 5 ft., one creature. *Hit*: 10 (3d6) necrotic damage. The target must succeed on a DC 10 Constitution saving throw or its hit point maximum is reduced by an amount equal to the damage taken. This reduction lasts until the creature finishes a long rest. The target dies if this effect reduces its hit point maximum to 0.

The players have two options here. The specter will not attack them unless provoked. If they wait and speak to it, the specter will warn them away from the game before opening the door for them.

> **The specter as an NPC:** It is a miserable, ghostlike creature that sets the room aglow. It's tired. It doesn't want to fight, but it will if you make it. It doesn't particularly care if you go through the game, but it warns you away anyway. It only tries once.

If the players choose to speak to the specter, it will tell them that the whole game is a trap. Many of the enemies you will face once had the hope you do, and all of them had those hopes dashed. You will not find the treasure you seek within. Go back now. Go back.

There is no option but to go forward, and the specter will open the door for them if they simply ask. They may fight it, but they aren't meant to. It's no danger to them. Once they fight it or ask for the door to be opened, the specter will open the door to reveal a spiral staircase of carved marble. The game begins.

2: Labyrinth

The players make their way through the doorway, and they can almost hear the specter cackling as they descend the stairs and enter the game. There is another amber glowing inscription on the wall a few steps in front of them.

Trap 1

A rogue should check for traps before they set foot in the labyrinth. Rolling for Perception (DC 15) should also reveal the first trap—or at least that something is off. The first trap will be in the entryway. The floor is made of individual marble blocks, but there is one jet black block in the entryway. Stepping on that block will press it down and trigger a spike to come up through the floor, dealing 1d10+3 piercing damage. Successful Investigation (Int) DC 12 will disarm. Save DC 10.

After stepping around the trap or springing it, the players will be able to read the inscription.

> To earn the treasure that you seek,
> my labyrinth you must defeat.
> One wrong turn and bones will break—
> play my game and tempt your fate.

Skeletons

There are a couple correct paths through the labyrinth. At many wrong turns, the players may run into skeletons. Unlike the specter, they will be unable to reason with these undead. Each of the skeletons they will find in the labyrinth are others who attempted the game and failed. Paeor keeps them hostile.

Skeleton

Medium undead, lawful evil
Armor Class 13 (armor scraps)
Hit Points 13 (2d8 + 4)
Speed 30 ft.

STR	DEX	CON	INT	WIS	CHA
10 (+0)	14 (+2)	15 (+2)	6 (-2)	8 (-1)	5 (-3)

Damage vulnerabilities bludgeoning
Damage Immunities poison
Condition Immunities exhaustion, poisoned
Senses darkvision 60 ft., passive Perception 9
Languages understands the languages it knew in life but can't speak
Challenge 1/4 (50 XP)

Actions

Shortsword. *Melee Weapon Attack*: +4 to hit, reach 5 ft., one target. *Hit*: 5 (1d6 + 2) piercing damage.
Shortbow. *Ranged Weapon Attack*: +4 to hit, range 80/320 ft., one target. *Hit*: 5 (1d6 + 2) piercing damage.

Skeletons 1–3 are on the main path through the labyrinth. All others can be avoided by taking the correct path.

Adjusting the Encounters: Skeletons are numbered on the map. All skeletons will remain, but for weaker parties, they will just be piles of bones instead of foes.

—Very weak: use skeletons 1–3.
—Weak: use skeletons 1–5.
—Strong: use skeletons 1–7.
—Very strong: use skeletons 1–10.

Trap II

This trap may be avoided by taking the correct path. This is a traditional arrows-in-the-wall trap. There is another tell-tale sign here: the same black stone is the trigger. Stepping on the black stone will cause crossbow bolts to be shot at the player from the end of the long hallway. Tripping the trap causes 1d10+3 piercing damage. Successful Investigation (Int) DC 12 will disarm. Save DC 10. By this, players may also notice the pattern with the black tiles and fall back on passive Perception.

Trap III

Like Trap II, this trap may be avoided by taking the correct path. This is another traditional arrows-in-the-wall trap. The same black stone is the trigger. Stepping on the black stone will cause crossbow bolts to be shot at the player from the wall to the right (between X_3 and S_4). Tripping the trap causes 1d10+3 piercing damage. Successful Investigation (Int) DC 12 will disarm. Save DC 10.

Darkmantle

There is one darkmantle in this room, lying in wait above a supply box in a small area off one of the wrong paths in the labyrinth.

Darkmantle

Small monstrosity, unaligned

Armor Class 11
Hit Points 22 (5d6 + 5)
Speed 10 ft., fly 30 ft.

STR	DEX	CON	INT	WIS	CHA
16 (+3)	12 (+1)	13 (+1)	2 (-4)	10 (+0)	5 (-3)

Skills Stealth +3
Senses blindsight 60 ft., passive Perception 10
Challenge 1/2 (100 XP)

Echolocation. The darkmantle can't use its blindsight while deafened.
False Appearance. While the darkmantle remains motionless, it is indistinguishable from a cave formation such as a stalactite or stalagmite.

Actions

Crush. *Melee Weapon Attack:* +5 to hit, reach 5 ft., one creature. *Hit:* 6 (1d6 + 3) bludgeoning damage, and the darkmantle attaches to the target. If the target is Medium or smaller and the darkmantle has advantage on the attack roll, it attaches by engulfing the target's head, and the target is also blinded and unable to breathe while the darkmantle is attached in this way. While attached to the target, the darkmantle can attack no other creature except the target but has advantage on its attack rolls. The darkmantle's speed also becomes 0, it can't benefit from any bonus to its speed, and it moves with the target. A creature can detach the darkmantle by making a successful DC 13 Strength check as an action. On its turn, the darkmantle can detach itself from the target by using 5 feet of movement.

Darkness Aura (1/Day). A 15-foot radius of magical darkness extends out from the darkmantle, moves with it, and spreads around corners. The darkness lasts as long as the darkmantle maintains concentration, up to 10 minutes (as if concentrating on a spell). Darkvision can't penetrate this darkness, and no natural light can illuminate it. If any of the darkness overlaps with an area of light created by a spell of 2nd level or lower, the spell creating the light is dispelled.

Players may roll for Perception (DC 15) to see if they spot the creature hanging from the ceiling. If not or if they fail, walking up to the box will cause the darkmantle to drop and attack. Defeating the darkmantle and opening the supply box will reveal one bottle of red liquid—potion of healing (2d4+2 HP)—per player.

Successfully navigating the labyrinth will bring the players to another spiral staircase.

3: Supply Room

This is a simple room without much to offer. It is intended to put the adventurer at ease and make them think there's a reward for them there. There isn't. Players simply need to cross this room to Room 4.

Trap IV

The whole room has a long, black path along the floor, straight down the middle from door to door. Walking along the black line will trigger a trap at the center of the hallway. Five seconds after stepping on the trigger, wooden spears jab out of the walls on either side, dealing 1d10+5 piercing damage to all players in the wide portion of the hallway. Successful Investigation (Int) DC 12 will disarm. Save DC 10.

Darkmantles

There are two possible darkmantles in this room. All players will encounter D_2 if they investigate those supply boxes. The darkmantle in the doorway drops when players try to open the door.

Supply Crates

The point of the supply room is to get you to investigate all the boxes and be disappointed. One random crate stack does hold one potion of healing per player (2d4+2 HP), but not the one with the darkmantle above it.

Once the players are satisfied and ready to move on, they need to cross the room and open the double doors to Room 4.

4: Deep Monsters

Upon entering Room 4, the players will be face to face with an unknown creature. There is nothing in this room besides the creature and its companion(s).

Molemask

The molemask is a typically peaceful burrowing creature that was created for Ambergrove. The molemask is humanoid in the daytime on the surface, mole in the daytime underground, and hybrid at night or when threatened. As another burrowing creature, it works well with the badgers. Stats are similar to wererats in D&D.

Molemask

Medium humanoid (shapechanger), unaligned
Armor Class 12
Hit Points 33 (6d8 + 6)
Speed 30 ft.

STR	DEX	CON	INT	WIS	CHA
10 (+0)	15 (+2)	12 (+1)	11 (+0)	10 (+0)	8 (-1)

Skills Perception +2, Stealth +4
Damage Immunities bludgeoning, piercing, and slashing from nonmagical attacks not made with silvered weapons
Senses darkvision 60 ft. (rat form only), passive Perception 12
Languages Common (can't speak in mole form unless using animal language)
Challenge 2 (450 XP)

Shapechanger. The molemask can use its action to polymorph into a mole-humanoid hybrid or into a giant mole, or back into its true form, which is humanoid. Its statistics, other than its size, are the same in each form. Any equipment it is wearing or carrying isn't transformed. It reverts to its true form if it dies.
Keen Smell. The molemask has advantage on Wisdom (Perception) checks that rely on smell.

Actions

Multiattack (Humanoid or Hybrid Form Only). The molemask makes two attacks, only one of which can be a bite.
Bite (Mole or Hybrid Form Only). *Melee Weapon Attack*: +4 to hit, reach 5 ft., one target. *Hit*: 4 (1d4 + 2) piercing damage.
Shortsword (Humanoid or Hybrid Form Only). *Melee Weapon Attack*: +4 to hit, reach 5 ft., one target. *Hit*: 5 (1d6 + 2) piercing damage.
Hand Crossbow (Humanoid or Hybrid Form Only). *Ranged Weapon Attack*: +4 to hit, range 30/120 ft., one target. *Hit*: 5 (1d6 + 2) piercing damage.

The party will encounter the molemask in hybrid form, and the molemask will remain in this form throughout the encounter.

In hybrid form, it has a humanoid stature, clawed hands, and a mole head. Its broad shoulders and barrel chest are direct from the mole's strong-digger musculature.

There is no way to avoid initial combat with the molemask or badgers. The players will be unfamiliar with the molemask being at this time, so they may not know they are typically peaceful. Players will have the option to kill or spare the being once defeated.

The molemask is experiencing long-term madness at the hands of Paeor. If a cleric uses *calm emotions*, he may turn to his human form and disappear with a smile. If they choose to spare him, he will be freed by Paeor at the end.

Giant Badger

The molemask is flanked by 1 giant badger—2 giant badgers for strong or very strong parties. The Ranger may try to speak to the giant badgers with Animal Handling (Wis) DC 20. Ordinarily, they could be talked down, just as ordinarily the molemask is a peaceful shifter. They are being controlled by Paeor, and there is no reasoning with them. You may choose to defeat the badgers and spare their lives or kill them.

Giant Badger

Medium beast, unaligned
Armor Class 10
Hit Points 13 (2d8 + 4)
Speed 30 ft., burrow 10 ft.

STR	DEX	CON	INT	WIS	CHA
13 (+1)	10 (+0)	15 (+2)	2 (-4)	12 (+1)	5 (-3)

Senses darkvision 30 ft., passive Perception 11
Challenge 1/4 (50 XP)

Keen Smell. The badger has advantage on Wisdom (Perception) checks that rely on smell.

Actions

Multiattack. The badger makes two attacks: one with its bite and one with its claws.
Bite. *Melee Weapon Attack*: +3 to hit, reach 5 ft., one target. *Hit*: 4 (1d6 + 1) piercing damage.
Claws. *Melee Weapon Attack*: +3 to hit, reach 5 ft., one target. *Hit*: 6 (2d4 + 1) slashing damage.

Once the players have defeated the creatures and decided what to do with them, they will be able to proceed down the final spiral stair.

5: Paeor

To disorient the players, the stair will shift while they descend, by Paeor's design. The spiral changes directions as they go. When the players have descended the stair, they will see a man sitting in a marble throne with large, marble braziers on either side of him. He is lanky with shaggy blond hair and bright blue eyes. Leaning casually in his throne, his blue plaid pants and vest are in full view.

Paeor as an NPC: He always wears something ridiculous, so he isn't taken seriously. It adds to the trick. When he speaks, it is thick with condescension.

Trap V

The final trap is sprung by standing on any of the stones just inside the doorway. Players can avoid the trap by jumping over it if detected, but this does not have a visual indicator aside from slightly raised blocks. Stepping on the trigger will cause the stairs behind the party to collapse. This blocks their exit. No one will be injured either way.

Trickster's Riddle

When the players step into the room, Paeor grins. He tells them that they should be proud to have made it so far in his game. All they will need to do to be victorious is to correctly answer his riddle.

Paeor asks the players what makes him the greatest of all the gods.

Options:

—If the players answer incorrectly (by providing any answer), Paeor will fight them for having lost.

—If the players decline to answer, that is the correct response. There is no right answer where a trickster is involved. Angry, he fights them anyway.

From the book:

> *"Paeor demanded they solve a riddle. He told them if they completed the riddle, they would be freed and the deep would be closed forever. The human knew better than to guess, for there could be no correct answer where a trickster was involved. He advised your father so, and Toren gave this answer to Paeor. The god became irate at losing the game. . . . Toren fought Paeor."* (*Ranger's Odyssey*, 33)

The Encounter

The players cannot avoid fighting Paeor. If they answer incorrectly, he will be overjoyed to fight them, but as soon as there is some response to the riddle, the encounter will begin.

Paeor

Medium humanoid (Trickster God), any chaotic alignment

Armor Class 17 (splint)
Hit Points 58 (9d8 + 18)
Speed 30 ft.

STR	DEX	CON	INT	WIS	CHA
16 (+3)	13 (+1)	14 (+2)	10 (+0)	11 (+0)	10 (+0)

Saving Throws Con +4
Skills Athletics +5, Perception +3

Senses passive Perception 13
Languages Common, all humanoid
Challenge 3 (700 XP)

Martial Role. *Attacker.* Paeor gains a +2 bonus to attack rolls.
Second Wind. Paeor can use a bonus action on its turn to regain 13 hit points. If it does so, it can't use this feature again until it finishes a short or long rest.
Improved Critical. The warrior's attack rolls now score a critical hit on a roll of 19 or 20 on the d20.

Actions
Multiattack. The trickster makes two longsword attacks. If it has a shortsword drawn, it can also make a shortsword attack.
Longsword. *Melee Weapon Attack*: +4 to hit, reach 5 ft., one target. *Hit*: 6 (1d8 + 2) slashing damage, or 7 (1d10 + 2) slashing damage if used with two hands.

There is no adjustment for this encounter. Having reached this point is enough. If the players are losing their fight with Paeor, Aeun will step in to help. If not, they will defeat Paeor on their own, and Aeun will appear.

From the book:

> *"Injured and losing, he asked Aeun for help. She appeared with Maonna and Daeda—our mother goddess and father god—and together they took Paeor back to their isles, closing the deep and giving Toren a badger token to prove his victory over Paeor."* (*Ranger's Odyssey*, 33)

Once the battle is over—one way or the other—the resolution will begin. The players can defeat Paeor, but they cannot kill him.

The Fates of the Fallen

Aeun, the goddess of the forest dwarves, appears in the chamber with the mother goddess, Maonna, and the father god, Daeda. They tell Paeor that the Ranger trial is binding, as are his promises to those who entered his game and perished. The souls of those who perished must be set free.

The players will see a hooded figure appear beside the other deities, and all the skeletons they faced will appear beside the figure in ghostlike form. The beings nod to the party, and then they all fade away.

The molemask is a person taken captive from Modoc. If they choose to spare the molemask, Daeda will leave to fetch him and take him away to be returned to his former self. He will also set the badgers free. If they were killed, these beings also appear in ghostlike form to be taken away.

Maonna takes Paeor, and she disappears. Left alone, Aeun congratulates the Ranger on the completion of the trial. Toren is given a token from Aeun—a badger—and then he is awarded the title of Ranger of Aeunna. Aeun takes them to the surface, and then the opening to Paeor's game collapses before their eyes. It is over.

Conclusion

Upon completion of the trial, Toren returns to the people of Modoc and those who prepared to build Nimeda, to tell them they had nothing more to fear. Paeor had been defeated.

The humans thanked Toren for the service he had done them, and the people of Nimeda would erect a statue in his honor.

The successful completion of Paeor's game also served to introduce Toren to Dakota's daughter, Kenda, who would become his wife and Mara's mother. Their union would ensure that a prophecy would be set in motion and Ambergrove would be forever changed. But that is another story.

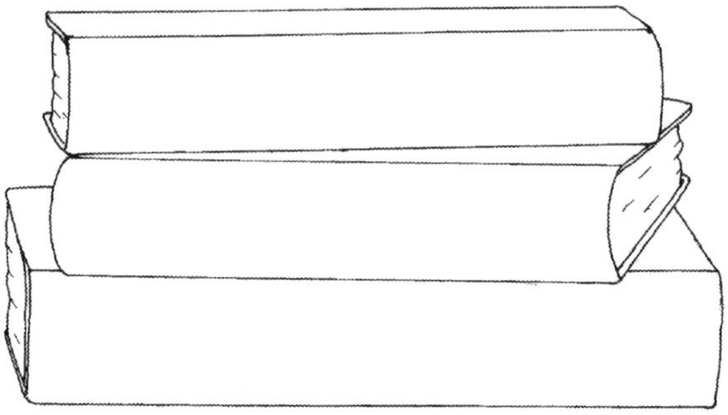

Rewards

Make sure if these characters will be played again that rewards are noted on player logsheets. In addition to the below standards rewards, as a story reward, the Ranger has completed their trial and can now lead the forest dwarves.

Experience

Total all combat experience earned for defeated foes and divide by the number of characters present and surviving the combat. Non-combat experience should be counted by character. All players receive **200 base XP.**

$$200 + [\text{non-combat}] + ([\text{combat}] \div [\text{party members}])$$

Combat

Name of Foe	XP per Foe
Specter	200
Skeleton	50
Darkmantle	100
Molemask	450
Giant badger	50
Paeor	700

Non-Combat

Task or Accomplishment	XP per Character
Do not fight the specter	50
Disarm/miss trap 1	25
Disarm/miss trap 2	25
Disarm/miss trap 3	25
Disarm/miss trap 4	25
Disarm/miss trap 5	25
Spot at least 1 darkmantle	50
Try to speak to badgers	75
Spare molemask	100
Spare badgers	100
Answer the riddle correctly	75

Treasure

Although there is no formal treasure, some supply boxes and encounters provided rewards. Characters should attempt to divide treasure evenly or by need wherever possible. If group is unable to decide, DM may select randomly.

Treasure	GP Value
Potions of healing (2ea)	50
Shortsword +1	500
Ruby (2)	1000
Token of Aeun	—

Renown

For successfully completing the game, players earn one renown point.

Favors and Enmity

The characters have the opportunity to earn the following during play.

Favor of Nimeda and Modoc. You defeated Paeor and ended the game. This has earned you the favor of all the humans you have saved from both villages. So long as you have this favor, all future Charisma (Deception, Intimidation, or Persuasion) made against gnomish guards are made with advantage.

Author's Note

Thank you for playing the Ambergrove adventures and delving further into this world! D&D has been a huge part of my life for as long as I can remember. My parents played AD&D with my aunts and uncles in college and later when they were building their families. I played with them when I was a teenager. I read the Dragonlance and Forgotten Realms books and loved to just sit on the floor by the bookshelves and flip through the core books.

No matter how many iterations there are or what other RPGs hit the market, there will always be a timelessness and charm from classic D&D.

There will always be people who gather around the tabletop and imagine adventures. The *clickety-clack* of the goblins' many dice sets will always be melodious to some. There will always be those who are held, transfixed, by the story woven by a fantastic DM, and there will be others who simply smile pleasantly as a baby DM trudges on.

Because there's love at that table too.

There's joy in the characters who are meant to be fun *and* the characters who are meant to be fierce. There's joy in the adventure.

In *Ranger's Odyssey*, I begin the book with a quick immersion into a D&D session. I used two of my parents' old characters—Dalzi and Danag—as the player characters.

While there was never an escape from my mom or sibling in going off to play D&D, because we all did it together, some of those first few pages ring true. I greatly shortened the original play group between drafts. I'd previously included everyone I grew up with, all the family I'd played with, but I ended up cutting things down to avoid spending too much time on characters we wouldn't see again. But what is real is that feeling of giddiness and pure, unbridled joy at the thought of going to see this found family.

One of my earliest memories as a child was my uncle walking into my parents' house with crates of core books and DM supplies.

Would I have come around to fantasy without that group who took turns playing AD&D on couches in each of their living rooms, whose DM made a felted table that I'd see every time I went downstairs growing up? Without my dad's extensive journals through the eyes of Daldar or Dalzi between adventures? Without the legends of Garon or Dammit? Maybe.

Would my life be as rich if we hadn't dusted off that old, felted table and set it up for my generation of players in my own home? Certainly not.

There's a magic in this game that has nothing to do with spell slots. I hope you continue to experience that magic for years to come. May your dice roll in your favor. May your player schedules line up. May you feel the love like I did. May it take you on the grandest of adventures.

Printed in the United States
by Baker & Taylor Publisher Services